AMNESIA IN A REPUBLICAN COUNTY

Amnesia in a Republican County

A Novel by

GARY SOTO

UNIVERSITY OF NEW MEXICO PRESS

★

ALBUQUERQUE

Library of Congress Cataloging-in-Publication Data

Soto, Gary.
  Amnesia in a Republican county / Gary Soto.— 1st ed.
    p. cm.
  ISBN 0-8263-2931-4 (cloth : alk. paper)
  1. Mexican American poets—Fiction. 2. College teachers—Fiction.
3. California—Fiction. 4. Amnesia—Fiction. I. Title.

PS3569.O72 A83
813'.54—dc21

                                                        2002011203

Design: Mina Yamashita

To Andrew Tonkovich

and Lisa Alvarez

Who Know

Books by Gary Soto

Amnesia in a Republican County
Poetry Lover
The Effects of Knut Hamsun on a Fresno Boy
Jessie De La Cruz: A Profile of a United Farm Worker
Nickel and Dime
A Natural Man
Nerdlandia
Buried Onions
Junior College
New and Selected Poems
Jesse
Pieces of the Heart: New Chicano Fiction
Home Course in Religion
Who Will Know Us?
A Summer Life
A Fire in My Hands
California Childhood
Lesser Evils
Small Faces
Black Hair
Living Up the Street
Where Sparrows Work Hard
The Tale of Sunlight
The Elements of San Joaquin

Amnesia in a Republican County

Chapter One

Veteran Chicano poet Silver Mendez rose to his knees, two knobs of cartilage worn out not from Catholic genuflection, but by the higher, no-nonsense order of the police. He unsteadily grabbed the edge of a desk. He moaned and touched his temple for the pulse of a headache in full stride. An ancient IBM typewriter had fallen on his head when he reached for a dictionary, something he hadn't done in years because he hadn't written a poem in god-knows-how-long. He wasn't aware that he had grabbed a dictionary, or that the shelf it had rested on had collapsed, sending the typewriter falling on a collision course with his head. No, Silver was suffering from amnesia, but as he rose unsteadily to his feet, he had it in his mind that he had just woken up with a *cruda*, a nasty hangover. What else could it be?

"How much did I drink?" he muttered. He smacked his lips and thought he could taste a dry, furry sock, the usual texture of his tongue after a night out. Oiled by a flash flood of tears, his eyes swung wildly in their sockets. He closed his peepholes until the swinging stopped.

He scanned his environs, one hand gripping the desk, afraid his buckling legs would send him once again to the floor. He didn't recognize this office lined with books from floor to ceiling. For a split second, the room seemed like the dusty hollow of a lawyer's office, but Silver couldn't recall a specific crime that would have sent him there. Indeed he had been in and out of the drunk tank, had had batons cracked all around his dented skull, was frisked for stolen goods and drugs, and was forced to obey a restraining order filed against him— this done by a dog, or on the dog's behalf by his girlfriend at the time. She was doing three months for passing bad checks and didn't want him to claim their pooch.

Silver shook his head, but stopped that action when a headache claimed precedence over his awareness of events, such as it was. He held his head in his hands and cried, "Shit," a word he would later remember was employed in a good many of his early poems. But the echo of that foul word disturbed his balance, so he remained quiet. As he inspected the room, he realized that it resembled a professor's cage. He trailed a finger along a dusty shelf of books. Who would pretend to have read so much? Plus, a portrait of shaggy-bearded Walt Whitman was peering down at him. Like the old, queer poet with his belly full of warmth and good living, Silver hung a beard on his face, a fetish that he gripped for reassurance when he was in trouble. And he appeared in trouble at the moment. His head hurt and he had no idea where he was.

Silver shifted his attention to another portrait: James Joyce with an eye patch.

What you looking at, man? he would have asked, but feared the bong of blood in his brain would spill out of his nose and ears. He took things slowly. Head throbbing, he sat carefully down in a swivel chair and closed his eyes for a little R & R. His head hurt in an immense way. His eyes slowly peeled open after the pain receded into whatever chamber of the brain manufactures such suffering as headaches and sour moods. He would have sought an answer to the broken typewriter on the floor. But he warned himself: Dude, take it easy. He was scared his curiosity might generate a greater pain. He counted his breaths, grateful that his chest still rose and fell, grateful that the light of the day still penetrated his eyes and that he had not been called earthward into death. Still, he was confused. Just where was he? He cupped a hand around his mouth and blew: no scent of booze, neither of the soft nor hard kind. He blew a second time: no sweet smell of *mota* either. Silver was reduced to a state of confusion.

He rose from the chair and bent over a black institutional telephone from the 1970s. The number on the dial wasn't familiar. He looked at the framed pictures on the desk: two were of a family, all blonde, and the third was a faraway snapshot of a man holding up a large and out-of-luck trout. There were paperweights, cast in bronze and shaped into ducks, plus an ashtray, a herd of paper clips, a stapler, and a calendar opened to September and the proclamation: Gone fishin'.

"What the fuck is this about?" Silver asked the air.

The sunlight brutally attacked his senses when the door of the office was flung open and a young man rushed in unannounced. Breathing hard, he fluttered a piece of typing paper at Silver. For a moment, Silver tried to connect the typewriter on the floor and the typing paper in the young man's hands. When his head started to hurt, he let the thought go. He slowly sized up the young man, his face studded with metal parts, a fashion the young would regret thirty years later when the holes in their aged faces still remained. The young man's hair was purple, though underneath Silver could see that it had been orange at one time, perhaps last week.

"It's all done, professor!" the young man exclaimed proudly. His chest was heaving, his smile pulled to full mast.

Professor?

"I did what you told me to do," the young man said. His smiled relaxed, then widened. "I had a little smoke before I wrote."

"A little smoke?" Silver mused. A cloud seemed to sail across the surface of his pupils.

The young man shoved the poem toward Silver's face, the whiteness of the typing paper reminding Silver of a flapping seagull.

"Can you read it, Professor?"

Silver clutched the poem and examined it briefly before he placed it on the desk and inquired, "Where are we?" Silver was still shaky. Most of his memory had apparently gone down the drain, although he knew he was Silver Mendez, a poet. Then a second flash lit his memory: he was from Oakland, he owned a Volkswagen up on cement blocks, and his mother, a woman with scalded hands and a temper that matched her occupation, worked in an industrial laundry, washing the duds of convicts in the Alameda County Jail. For reasons he couldn't understand, these truths hurt. To block them from his memory, he mumbled weakly a second time, "Where are we and who are you?"

The young man giggled. His giggling revealed a chrome ball on his tongue. "Professor Mendez, you know I can't answer large questions like those."

Silver blinked. "You don't know where you are? Who you are?"

The young man's enthusiasm disappeared. "I told you my dad was a missionary and moved around a lot when I was a kid." He appeared troubled, a wedge of wrinkles deepening around the bridge of his nose. "Plus, like you said in class, we don't know where we're going and so, like, how do I know where I am? Or who I am?"

Silver became baffled. What class? He turned and peered up at Walt Whitman, but the poet didn't offer any hints. He glanced over at a framed picture of people he didn't know: they were all smiling—laughing righteously?—at him. Some of this had to make sense. He touched the poem on the desk and noted that it was titled "Puff" and dedicated "To Jenny." But his interest was not in the poem but in discovering his whereabouts. Absently, he put his hands into his pockets and felt the jagged edges of a key and a second key on a chain. He brought the keys from his pocket and considered them for a moment, especially the key chain that stated, in Old English script, "Jesus Loves You." He shoved them back into his pocket.

"What the fuck is this about?" Silver asked. He spread his feet widely, as if the answer might knock him to the floor.

The young man believed the question pertained to his poem, since it was poorly typed and perhaps somewhat mysterious as it was composed all in capitals and, to the untrained eye, resembled a lunatic's ransom note. His hurt disappeared, and with it, the lines around his brow. "I knew it was good," he crowed, rocking on the heels of his boots, still shiny at the tips because he had yet to traverse the world. "Like you said, 'Write not from your brain or heart but from your throat.'" He also reminded Silver that he had said a poem didn't have to mean a whole lot as long as the composer was sincere at the moment of its creation.

The thesis sounded vaguely familiar to Silver. Then he remembered—some more of his past was coming back—that he had pronounced this opinion a number of times, usually in bars with other unemployed poets tainted with the smell of cigarettes and unwashed hair. By this, he meant that a poet's role was to shout his or her convictions so that corporate America would wake up to a Chicano reality. And as for meaning, well, all words counted toward the sum of what a writer was getting at; this, too, however, was not wholly important. What was important was keeping people in their chairs when you started to read your stuff.

"I'm going to ask you again," Silver said seriously. He rose unsteadily to his feet. He placed his hands on the young man's shoulders and looked him in the eye. "Where in the fuck are we?"

The office became quiet. The distance between them—professor and student—widened.

Nearly blubbering, the young man tried to step backward, but Silver held his soft shoulders firmly. When Silver shook him, tears like dimes spilled to the floor, an expensive loss because the young man produced a wet frown. Silver scolded, "Where are we, dude?"

The young man wiped his nose with the heel of his palm and bent down as if to gather the coinage of his spilled tears—a folded piece of paper had fallen from his shirt pocket. He righted himself and faced up to a truth: "I don't know where we are, Professor, but I think it might be hellsville if I don't get at least a B+ for the semester."

Silver let his arms fall from the young man's shoulders. Right then, he knew he must be teaching at a state college.

★

After the student left with his shoulders sloped from disappointment, Silver rifled through the drawers and discovered that he was using the office of one Professor Joshua Petersen, who was on sabbatical. The note "gone fishin'" made sense when Silver came across a jar of salmon eggs in a zip-lock bag. There were also a number of magazines devoted to fly-casting. Two fishing rods collapsed like scaffolding when he pulled open the closet door.

Silver also learned that the professor was a poet with two books under his belt—the mug on the back of one of his books matched the one with the family and the single trout. He scanned one poem titled "Autumn." The figure in the poem was perched on a rock sniveling over a lost summer when he had a coed in his arms but let her go without exploring the virtues of her youthful breasts. Silver meditated on whether to throw the book against the wall. He had lost something far more precious than time and a coed—his memory, admittedly full of holes from the drinking of tall cold ones and sparking up of joints with riffraff in the summer of his youth. Then again, he might have lost some of his zest when he gorged himself on too many mushrooms back in 1978. This much Silver remembered about himself. But Silver was careful not to trigger a warranted outburst. He feared that his head, still spinning, might burst open.

Silver touched the top of his scalp and tasted his fingertips, which were sticky as jam. He did not think that he could have oozed so much blood, thin as he was. At 5'9", he weighed only 135 pounds, and much of that weight involved his beard, long hair, and his belt buckle shaped into the Brown Power clenched fist. But the blood flow had stopped and he was alive, though the wires in his brain that conducted memory might be a bit frayed. He peered out the window blinds. There were hundreds of students dressed in slacks and skirts. Some of the young men sported ties, and the young women purses on their shoulders. Silver wondered: Is it the fifties? He imagined that the Beav and Wally might appear, books in their hands. He was encouraged when he thought he spotted a rebel wobbling by on a scooter until he saw the Bush/Cheney sticker on his briefcase.

"Where am I?" he asked himself again.

While no geographer, he suspected that he must be teaching at a desert college, for none of the students wore sweaters or coats. They were dressed lightly. He looked down at his clothes: faded bell-bottom cords, a faded shirt, and huarache sandals, the kind that the lowlifes of Christ's time might have envied. He saw that one purplish toenail was poking out of its sock.

When the telephone rang, Silver flinched. He hesitated before answering it, but on the sixth ring, he picked it up and held it a foot from his ear. Nevertheless, he heard a gruff voice on the other end ask, "Where are you?"

Good question.

The question was followed by breathing, then the repeated question, "Where are you?" though this time the speaker added with spice, "Motherfucker."

Unwilling to get involved with such a nasty tele-marketer, Silver hung up. He patted the back of his pants and pulled out his wallet, which confirmed what he remembered about himself: that he was Silver Mendez of Oakland, California, was a poet, and was a holder of two expired library cards, a stick of Juicy Fruit gum, a receipt for articles left at the Rescue Mission in Richmond, and six dollars as wrinkled as his clothes. There was also a circular dent where he had once kept a condom, just in case. But for him, "just in case" never arrived and the condom had to be thrown away, the date long expired.

He had the brain power to recall his name was, but the

question of how he got such a cushy position—professor at a
state college, a sabbatical replacement for a poet who wrote
about rivers and middle-class loneliness, for instance—was at
the forefront of his worry. Try as he might he couldn't put
two and two together. He was aware that he had a Volkswagen
and a mother, this much he knew from the previous recall.
Then he chanted the mantra of "home, home, home." The
image of home indeed appeared: he pictured a sagging bed, a
single chair, a sputtering candle, and a rope twisted into a
noose. Was that right? Was that home? He then filled his
memory with the smoke of *frijoles* burning on the back burner.

The telephone rang again, blowing away the frightening
images of his home life. The nasty telemarketer? This time,
however, Silver didn't jump, for he was peeved but coolly
peeved. He slowly raised the telephone to his ear. "Yeah,
motherfucker, but do you know where you are?"

The voice was female. "What?"

His anger drained. "Oh, I'm sorry." He immediately
brought a fingernail to his mouth and chewed nervously.

The female voice said firmly, "Silver, your class is waiting."

Silver pondered, class? Immediately, he remembered the
young man—missionary brat and versifier of poems in all
caps—and replied as he touched the top of his head, "I had a
little accident." He licked his lips and asked meekly, "Where
is my class?"

The female voice serenaded his ears with the name of
the building, the room number, and the thirty-three steps it
took to climb to the second floor. She hung up without a
good-bye, but not before saying, "You better not be late, you
hot tamale! I'm washed."

Hot tamale? I'm washed?

Silver set out from Professor Petersen's office with five books in his arms, as he assumed that he had to play the part of scholar-poet. The noontime heat was like a lance thrust into his chest. He sucked in hot air and ascertained by the harsh light that he must be in either Arizona or Texas, or maybe New Mexico. He was far from home and, from the look of things, might not make it back if his memory didn't kick start somewhere along the line.

Chapter Two

After a meandering trek through the campus that included stops at every corner of a tall hedge or building to inquire about the whereabouts of Baker Hall, Silver located the classroom. Rushing in, sweaty and furtive as a fox, he found three of the five students with their heads on their desks, as if lengthening their necks for an executioner. The other two stared straight ahead, eyes glazed over. Silver followed their stares to a large metaphysical o of a zero on the white board—a leftover symbol of a philosophy class? Or was that how they felt? Had they been depleted of wet yawns and were now coerced by boredom to gaze forward for an answer to the lateness of their professor?

"I'm sorry, but I was hog-tied after some cowpoke stole my watch," he quipped to his students. One responded with a yawn while another dabbed a finger at the corner of his eye, where a tear sprouted like a seed. Silver set the books on the table, a weight he was happy to relinquish. With a towel that hung from a hook, he erased the zero to get their attention.

"Less than a zero is a blank white board," he declared. He found his quip a daring piece of philosophy and promised to recall it when he cracked his knuckles and once again got busy writing poetry.

Slowly, each of the sleeping students raised his or her head and blinked sleepily in the artificial light of a modern classroom. Aroused, they rubbed their eyes and came alive, even the students who now shifted their attention from the white board to their professor. Their glazed look disappeared and smiles sprang up like flowers.

Silver shivered. The room, overly refrigerated, raised tribes of goose bumps on his arms. He hugged himself, but released his arms immediately because he didn't wish to give the students the impression that he liked himself. Poets never liked themselves, of that much he was certain. Some Irish types stood on the backs of spotted cows and hung themselves in barnyards. Some academic types ate until their breaths smelled perpetually of garlic and sour wine. Some English bards were so distraught by their failed efforts at minor masterpieces that they placed rocks in the pockets of their long Victorian skirts and walked bravely into rivers. Most poets, lazy as dogs, just grumbled about life's injustices, especially when the cigarette smoke around their faces cleared and they confronted temples of crushed beer cans and not a single cold one to be found.

A student in a cheerleader's outfit raised her hand.

"Yes?" Silver asked, struggling to keep his eyes from burning holes in her pinkish knees, which were parted slightly but not vulgarly, a white dove of a hand resting properly on her little, pleated skirt. Instead, he locked his attention on her eyes, clear and unused. He didn't know what lay behind her eyes—brilliance or knuckle-headed stupidity. Silver tugged at his beard. If you looked that clean and youthful, who cared?

"Jason left," she squealed. She informed him that Jason was too cold in the room to sit and write and instead took his poem to work on it outside. She pointed out the window. "There he is."

Everyone turned, two students pushing up tall as giraffes, and made out Jason on the lawn, T-shirt off but draped like a prayer shawl over his head. His legs were folded into a contorted yoga posture that would have killed an old man. A book lay at his side.

Silver didn't have to play the part of a giraffe by craning his neck. He was aware that the young poet was the student who had come to his office with the poem dedicated to a lass named Jenny. He was suddenly worried about the advice that he had plied on the student, something about stoking up a joint before composing a poem. God, if he could only remember what else he had advised. Silver gripped the desk as he winced through a sort of déjà vu experience that wobbled his knees. His head jolted as a piece of memory slid back into place. The memory was of himself as a young man with long hair sitting on a beanbag in a dark living room in East *Los*. He was writing a poem on the back of an envelope that contained an unpaid bill, while a stratum of smoke hung around his face. In the background, an Asian buddy of his was asleep, a bong the size of a beach ball in his arms. He shook his head and the vision wafted away like smoke.

"Should I go get him?" another student asked.

"Nah," Silver replied. "Let's get organized. I'll talk to—" Silver faltered. What was the kid's name again? Also, he didn't know any of the faces in his class and wasn't he supposed to be the teacher? He patted his back pockets as if his roll book were stuffed back there.

"Jason," the cheerleader filled in for her professor.

Silver thanked her with a smile. He noticed that her skirt was red and white and was curious why she was wearing such a getup. What kind of college was this where cheerleaders wrote poetry? But the answer to his question was of secondary importance as he deliberated how he was going to get their names out of them, his sloe-eyed students. He opted to be direct.

"Class," he began, then stopped as he licked his lips. He was perplexed why they seemed such attentive, upright citizens, the kind who, in time, would pair off and make babies and repeat themselves for another generation. "Class, I had an accident. A typewriter fell on my head and I lost my memory."

"Cool," one of the students remarked. "My tennis partner hit me with his racquet and I saw colors."

Silver frowned. A few renegade hairs jutted from his eyebrows like antennas. Then he lightened up as he seized upon the notion of a no-brainer day. He was aware for the first time that perhaps not being charged up with memory was not in itself a disability. This way he could get along in life without his childhood hang-ups, whatever they were, though he was certain that something tragic happened in the past—why else would he be standing in front of five students all better dressed than he? He glanced down at his feet; he dwelt on a toe presenting its pinkness through his sock, by no means a fashion faux pas among poets but a noticeable blunder in this class of well-dressed students. Silver told the class that he was speaking in metaphors and asked them if they knew what a metaphor was.

"Yeah," a student said confidentially. "It's when two things sort of, like, collide, but a person can't see because no two minds work alike." The student clacked his pen between the top and bottom rows of his bright teeth.

"No, it's like when parents divorce," another argued. "One goes one way and the other goes the other way."

Silver managed a grin, but behind the grin lay the perpetual question: Where in the fuck am I? Then he decided—what the hell—to be direct. "Ok, it sounds like a joke, but I trust all of you." He waited for them to lean forward in their chairs in the body language of friendship and trust. But none did. Still, he braved, "I'm going to have to ask, just where are we?"

Two of the students flipped open their binders as they prepared to take notes. They assumed their professor was speaking in metaphors and something snappy was about to be tossed in the air. Silver didn't know that on a previous meeting he had told the class that he had had an out-of-body experience that took him to the height of his childhood tree, a chinaberry, and he wasn't even loaded on any legal or illegal substance. From that height, he glimpsed his Father, and not a deadbeat pappy in front of the television, but a spiritual being who advised him to walk, not run, through life. The wise and good Father took his hand and showed him where three bushy marijuana plants perfumed the bank of a stinky canal outside of Fresno.

Silver sighed; they weren't getting that he was serious. He figured that after class he was just going to saunter to the front of the campus and read its name. He returned to his belated option of asking them if they had been writing new poems. Then a bit of brightness flashed inside his head. He beckoned the cheerleader for a piece of binder paper in order to take roll.

"Roll?" she asked. "There are only five of us here." She then swiveled her lovely head toward the window. "Plus Jason."

The students glanced at the window.

Silver remained firm. He stared at the cheerleader until she tore out a piece of binder paper, wrote her name in a large, looping script, and started the roll sheet circulating. Meanwhile, he began to talk about how poetry was a matter of breath and image, but that breath was far more important because it suggested life, and if you weren't alive then how did you expect to write poetry? He made other claims as well, all the while pacing in front of the class and praying that some but not all of his memory would hurry up and come back. He believed, though not strongly, that the teaching profession influenced youths in a positive manner. But good teachers were rare individuals. Most were scatterbrained lecturers, guilty of consumer fraud. He felt unprepared to teach his students. Once his memory booted itself back up with its original circuitry, he would apologize for his lack of consciousness and, if need be, inflate their grades slightly.

"It's done, Professor," a student said proudly, as if putting names on binder paper were an accomplishment.

Silver took the paper and studied it: two Ambers, two Chrises, two Jasons. He touched the top of his head, convinced that something was seriously wrong with the folds of his brain matter. Was he seeing double? Or was this Noah's ark?

"I wrote Jason's name down," a student volunteered. He was one of the kids who had taken a stab at defining a metaphor.

"Thanks, Chris," Silver risked.

"Nah, I'm Jason."

Silver blinked, then lowered his gaze to their names, all with the same ring of blandness. When the bell sounded, they gathered their books, but not before Silver asked that each of them turn in a poem by next class and, yes, to bring copies. While four students left class by the effort of their legs, a Chris or a Jason rode out on a scooter devouring a candy bar that rained flakes of chocolate with each bite.

★

It occurred to Silver that he could have asked one of the

students in the courtyard about the name and place of their college, but he had just escaped from appearing completely incompetent in front of his own students. Why take a chance with others? He could hear the rumors already: the prof with the scraggly beard, long, stringy hair, and outdated clothes doesn't know where he is. Hahaha.

With books in hand, Silver strode to what he believed was the front of the school, momentarily of the mind that knowledge weighed a person down—the books were cumbersome at a time when he needed to be fleet of foot. He stepped carefully into the flowerbed, sadly injuring a pretty-faced petunia, and parted a large, spiky juniper that stung his wrists. He regarded the name of the college stamped in a casket-shaped granite rock. In bronze letters, the sign read Simi Valley Baptist College. He tilted his face up and toward the main school building, which was half-church, half-Safeway in design. Organ music appropriate for the slowest marches droned from an open window. A single black bird made a ruckus on the wide lawn.

"Shit," Silver muttered, letting the books slip from his grip. He jumped from the flowerbed and stomped a jig to rid his sandals of the damp earth. He had assumed that he was in the Southwest, seeing that the sky was lit with a fiery sun and that the students were mostly white and well behaved, perhaps Republican beneath the veneer of their youthful rebellion of riding skateboards and scooters. He had also assumed that he was teaching at a state college—the first student he had met was begging for a better grade, a sure sign. But he was wrong on both accounts. He was in Blanche, California, in an area called Simi Valley, home of mostly honest taxpayers who had escaped none too quickly the mayhem of Watts and inner-city Los Angeles in the late 1960s. These were the people who kept neat lawns, fired up barbecues on weekends, and bought large television sets whose flickering lights lit up their walls with color.

In spite of the heat of the day—late afternoon, now that the sun was half-eclipsed by a line of fluttering eucalyptus—Silver shivered. His body's reaction was not a response to a passing cold front, but from his fear that he was in the wrong place. First, he wasn't Baptist, or Catholic for that matter, his religion being something more practical like praying for food and a clean bed. Second, as a flood of memories avalanched back into place, he seized upon the name of the college, the Simi Valley part. He recalled that the jurors in the trial that acquitted the police officers in the Rodney King case made their homes on the very earth he was trying to kick off his sandals. Memory or no memory, Silver was aghast that he had taken a job at a college so far from his principles, whatever they might be, though he believed that they were independent of consumerism as evidenced by a waistline that suggested that he seldom ate. Had he been so desperate?

Silver hurried back in the direction of his office, taking in the sites of the campus, which was mostly fertilized lawn, flower beds, crosses set here and there, a bronze statue of a stern-faced fellow in specs, and students on benches, some of whom had their Bibles open. Silver figured that his class—poetry writing—was probably the most radical of its sort. He stopped at a fountain, drank long and hard, and was jarred by the realization that with a college job a college paycheck most likely followed. How much was the institution paying him? And where was the English Department office? Maybe he could pick up his last paycheck and board a Greyhound bus and get out of town.

He then heard a voice rise up. "How come?"

Silver turned to find Jason, his student poet, still in his yoga posture. A man hovered above him, a Bible in his hand. The man, dressed in a blue suit, was shaking a finger at the youth and scolding him to put his T-shirt back on.

Silver commenced to tiptoe away, but he heard the youth bray accusingly, "There he is!" But Silver didn't heed the call, for in the past when he had responded with, say, "Yes, are you talking to me?" only bad things followed—more often than not, the police were accusing him of one crime or another. This much he remembered. Thus, his tiptoeing became a walk, then a skip, and finally an outright run when he heard "Professor Mendez!" echoing between the library and a tall, nondescript building that he would later learn was the chapel.

He made it to his office with his head throbbing. He felt for a spring of blood on his scalp. But when he touched the top of his head, he discovered only sweat. He rested in the swivel chair and breathed deeply until his ticker slowed and his eyelids lowered for a respite from the day's worries. The sweat stopped flowing and his worries receded like a headache. He was exhausted, but the fiery bush in his lungs continued to smolder. He picked up the photo of Professor Petersen's family. They were a happy group, possibly religious in their quest for more than a gassed-up SUV, or, in other words, a sumptuous middle-class living. They were probably asking for a place in the afterlife.

When the telephone rang, Silver picked up the receiver and put it back down. He repeated this action when the telephone rang again. Then a knock sounded, heavy and unkind, on his door. Silver froze. His heartbeat matched the repeated pounding. He took a step and the soles of his huaraches slapped against his feet. This tiny noise made the person start to bang furiously on the door.

"Who is it?" Silver braved.

"Who do you think it is?" asked a woman brusquely.

Silver opened the door, a slash of afternoon sunlight cutting across his chest. In bounded a well-dressed woman smelling of a mixture of cigarettes, perfume, and—Silver sniffed like a rabbit—photocopying. She was heavy-set, bejeweled, forty-something in real life but thirty-something among friends and acquaintances. She was a Latina with hips.

"Where were you?" she asked, followed up with, "How come you cussed at me?"

Silver bowed his head slightly as a migraine bullied itself to his frontal lobe. Was it from the typewriter—he noticed that it was still on the floor, a wreckage of sprung parts, a faded ribbon, and shattered keys—or was it from the woman who had just come in unannounced?

"I didn't cuss."

She raised her hands to her padded hips. Her head wagged when she cursed, "And 'motherfucker' ain't a cuss word?" She warned him that she was a Baptist of a moderate stripe (their sect allowed jewelry and makeup) and an employee of the college and knew all about lies and liars.

"Oh," Silver squeaked meekly. He remembered the voice on the telephone earlier. He remembered the voice saying, "Don't be late," and a lovey-dovey proclamation about his being a hot tamale. He lowered his head and pondered whether there was something truly wrong with him. Did he have lupus? A toothache that affected everything from his equilibrium to his male potency? A snarled artery in his neck that failed to feed him an adequate supply of fresh blood? He promised to get himself a physical at the Richmond Rescue Mission when he got back to the Bay Area. For now he raised his head, a new man, his shoulders square and true. He apologized, but didn't bother to explain why he had used such language. Also, he didn't have time to explain because she was frowning at the rubble of a broken typewriter on the floor.

"Oh, that," Silver said as he considered picking up the pieces from the floor. How did he know how it got there? It just did.

She burned a hole in his face. Then she softened and cooed. "If you weren't so good, I would walk out the door."

Good?

"My little poet with a long skinny thing," she mewed, her face inches from his own.

Long skinny thing?

She stepped away from Silver. She draped her purse across a chair, set a package on the floor, and started to undo her blouse, white as typing paper. In seconds, a lacy bra showed itself and the bra then hit the floor: two large breasts were presented to him, the nipples like hitchhiking thumbs.

"Ah," Silver managed to cry, though other words came to mind—"help" was one, and "mommy" was another.

"Come on, Daddy-O," she urged as she unhooked a skirt that puddled to the floor, exposing tree-trunk legs. She lowered her panties around her pudgy knees and then marched until they were kicked off.

"Wait a minute!" he warned without authority as he tottered backward and bumped into the desk. Who was this woman? Admittedly he was in awe of her breasts and curious at the depth of her shadowy navel. And her pubic hair did sparkle beneath the fluorescent light. Still, he demanded answers, but apparently was not about to get them. As he leaned away from her oncoming body, he toppled over the family photos of Professor Petersen.

"Please, wait a minute," he panted, trying to keep his knees together, an unlikely position even for a straight male without a memory.

"Don't you like it?" she asked after she released him, the beginning of a hickey darkening his pale throat. She stroked and parted his beard until it stuck like branches from his chin.

"I had an accident." Silver was breathing hard from fear. He pulled his beard back into its downward descent.

She eyeballed him.

"My memory is gone." He tried to look pathetic by pouting and considered the theatrics of rolling his eyeballs in their sockets.

She hesitated for a moment before she said, "So?"

She was on him, a hand like a crab on his crotch, her breasts smothering a plethora of words that he dearly wanted to get out, he being the poet with so much to say but no room to speak his mind at that moment. Instead, he obeyed the weight of her body: she had pressed him to the floor where he lay, like a good soldier, as she mounted him, her back to his face, the cargo of her mighty rump rising and falling on his half-stiff member. All the while, as she rode him to a Baptist ecstasy, he watched the shelf where the typewriter had crashed down. He feared other objects might fall and injure him for good.

Chapter Three

After this strange woman was appeased, Silver lay like driftwood, legs splayed and arms outstretched. His breathing slowed to a breathy "Oh, Oh, Oh." His back sparked with hurt from the hard floor, but not so painfully that he didn't mutter his praise to the woman—what was her name?—who knocked on his door and then knocked him down. He allowed his arms to swing over his head and his wrists to come together as if they were tied; his lean body was ready to be yanked up a wall for a bit of naughtiness. His hand touched a key from the broken typewriter. He fingered it and then raised it to his face: the key read "T." His eyelids fluttered closed and in a dreamy afterglow he witnessed again the breasts that might have been exhibit A if he had been smothered to death in their buttery loveliness. He smiled as he imagined a judge asking, "Breasts, can you tell us about the death of one Silvestre A. Mendez? Was it a matter of suffocation or pleasure in which the deceased expired?" Silver chuckled because he couldn't imagine a better exit from the dirty planet called earth. He released a final "Oh, Oh, Oh."

Then he experienced a jolt as a portion of his memory slid back into place: he pictured his roommate, Tyronne, back in Oakland, stabbing a finger into his chest and forming on his lips the ultimatum: "Silver, you gotta go!" Tyronne was furious, his eyes yellow as his teeth as he blasted away at Silver's failures, including a cutting remark about not flushing his stools. Their relationship had soured over money; Silver, bereft of his job as a groovy library aide because of state cutbacks, hadn't paid his share of the rent in three months and was unceremoniously shown the door. Silver hauled his belongings to his mother's place in Hayward, outpost for sons who couldn't do it on their own. Others his age—early forties, lean as convicts, gray-haired deadbeats with ponytails—would congregate in the public park for a talk, smoke, and little swigs from pint bottles the color of amber. All talked about getting jobs, but none made an effort to swing his legs into action and look.

Silver was searching his mind about whether he had a girlfriend back in Oakland when he felt himself yanked to his feet by the woman he assumed was his lover. His eyes were drawn to his member, soft as putty, and the shame of standing naked on a cold floor with portraits of Walt Whitman and James Joyce peering at him. Embarrassed, he would have covered his hand over his sticky genitals, but his lover still gripped his hands.

"Oh, my," she breathed, her hairdo collapsed to one side like the Leaning Tower of Pisa. "You're a real hot tamale."

"Thank you," Silver managed.

"Thank you?" his lover asked in return. She ruffled his hair and out came her tongue, which she slipped lizard-fast into Silver's mouth. After her tongue explored the inside of his mouth, she unlocked her face from his but kept an arm momentarily around his waist. But her arm, too, fell away. "You're so silly." She kicked up her panties with a toe and Silver caught them, the leg holes nearly as wide as his own waist. Silver presented them to her like flowers.

They dressed.

Silver worried about not knowing her name. He worried

how he had come to know her. From the look of things, he had only been teaching a couple of weeks. Did he get it on with her right away? And was she really Baptist? He was slipping into his shirt when she stopped him.

"I have a present for you."

"A present for me?" Silver loved presents.

From a bag she brought out a Hawaiian shirt and a new pair of sand-colored socks.

"Ah, that's great!" Silver sang as he pressed the shirt to his body. He tore off his own shirt and tossed it on the desk. He slipped into his new shirt, which fit loosely. But he told himself that that was the style in Hawaii, a one-size-fits-all sort of thing that allowed the islanders to pork out on Kalua pig and still look trim. He next pulled off his old socks and let them fall like banana peels into the wastebasket.

"I'm going to sneak a smoke," she said, letting the window blinds snap back. She had been scanning the courtyard where the faculty offices were situated and where students came to sit alone and meditate on their homework—the horse-shoe-shaped courtyard held stone and wooden benches and a hedge as tall as gallows. She plundered her purse for a pack of cigarettes and matches and exited, blowing a kiss at Silver in his new duds.

After the door closed, Silver swiftly pushed a hand in his lover's purse and brought out her wallet. He was tempted by the fives and tens, but was more interested in finding out her name. He was acquainted with her body—she had a big dipper of moles on the left cheek of her butt, for instance, and for all her weight and age her breasts didn't sag one bit. But he feared that she might go ballistic if he didn't call her by her given name. This was easily solved; he held her

California Driver's License in his hand: Laura Skaggs.

Skaggs?

Silver was flustered. By appearance and attitude, she was Latina to the core. Why the last name? But he didn't have time to sort that out. He shoved the license back into its compartment, the wallet into the purse, and the purse onto the desk where she had left it. Seconds later, she stepped back into the office, blowing a smoke ring that slowly widened into a hazy sombrero. The sombrero drifted toward his head, but he broke it apart with a wave of his hand. She did a playful tap dance and hugged Silver until he produced the cry of a beast caught under a log. She gave him three quick smooches and sucked the air from him with a long kiss.

"You ready?" Laura asked.

After he caught his breath and his nearly injured tongue became a regular working organ, Silver risked asking timidly, "Ready for what . . . Laura?"

She pushed him away and narrowed her eyes at him, a bull sighting its target. "Silver, what do you have— Alzheimer's? The game, for Christ's sake!"

The game?

For a moment Silver expected that he was going to have to strip his newly bought shirt and socks and do it again, perhaps in the same position, he on the bottom and she on top but facing him this time around. Was this what she meant by the game? If so, he had every intention of keeping on his socks, cozy little bunnies on his bony feet. He was also going to use the seat cushion in the chair to pillow his head.

"But there's a little gathering at our place first," Laura added, digging into her purse for a roll of breath mints. "Wesley expects us at five."

Gathering? Wesley?

Silver fixed his face with a perplexed look.

Laura caught the look. "The basketball game, you silly. Wesley, my husband!"

Silver's Hawaiian shirt filled with a blast: "Your husband!"

Laura's purse was now on her arm. She laughed. Her breath mint appeared on her tongue, flipping like a coin on the pink landscape. "Silly, and I thought you were so brave. You scared he might cut it off?" She made a pinching scissors motion with her left hand.

"You're married?"

"There is something wrong with you, isn't there?" Laura asked sincerely. She had pulverized her breath mint, and her tongue was coated white.

"Yeah, actually, there is," Silver admitted as he took a step backward. "I have to go home." Silver wasn't thinking about the place he called home here in Simi Valley—where was it, anyhow?—but back in Oakland. He envisioned himself running into the arms of Tyronne.

"Do you feel like writing a poem?" Laura brushed up against him and felt his forehead. "Are you in the poetry mood? Is that it?"

Was this what ordinary people thought when a person was confused? Silver shook his head. "Who's your husband anyhow?"

Laura pushed Silver away in order to make room to prop her hands on her hips.

"What?" Silver asked.

"How old are you? You sure you don't have Alzheimer's?" She softened as she took him into her arms and chuckled, the coolness of her minty breath freezing his ears. "Honey, he's your boss. The president of the college. Wesley."

Silver collapsed into a chair that gave up a mousy squeak. He had fooled and played the fool with other wives, but never with the wife of a college president. Had he picked the wrong college for such an activity? Didn't Baptists burn people? Or were they the ones that dunked people into rivers? He decided he would enrich his education by searching for an answer to that question after he got out of this mess.

Laura hopped onto Silver's lap, sidesaddle, and smoothed his hair. She nibbled his ear and praised his manly look in the Hawaiian shirt. She asked him to wiggle his toes and cooed that he was such a sweetie when, stuffed in their new socks, his toes pumped up and down. "I shouldn't have married so young. I should have had lots of lovers."

Silver wheezed, as she was a heavy load in his lap. "How old were you when you got married," he managed to ask.

"Eighteen."

Eighteen?

At that age he was still a pimple-faced lad playing with himself in the soapy waters of his bathtub.

"I was a virgin when I married. I didn't bleed, but I know I was a virgin." She kissed his neck and playfully fluttered her clumpy eyelashes against his cheek. "How about you? When did you first do it?"

Silver moaned under the heaviness of her flesh. He wasn't sure how long he could hold out. His cheeks became red, his breathing shallow.

"Fourteen."

She slapped his arm. "I knew it, you dirty boy! You started young. That's why you're so good!" She placed a long kiss on his lips, thus depriving him of precious air.

"When's this gathering?" he gasped after her mouth pulled away from his.

Laura leaped from his lap after she consulted with her watch. She peered out of the blinds to the courtyard smudged with shadows. She whispered, "I'll go first. Meet me in the parking lot." She left, her high heels rapping like gavels.

The gathering, it appeared, was right now.

★

As Silver made his way to the parking lot—the aura of overhead lights indicated its location—he took note that the college was small. Three large buildings of modern design were salmon-colored with tiled roofs and plenty of plate glass to enhance their importance. The library expressed the strength of steel and glass. When he passed its front foyer, his body grew in dimension in its mirrorlike reflection, his Hawaiian shirt gaudy and baggy on his thin body. His body widened into a square. He had the feeling that he was in the fun house at the county fair. Was he the major attraction?

He heard the tinkling music of a fountain in the distance. Organ music still resounded from a building. Sprinklers were dousing the lawns and flowerbeds, though it was already October in southern California. A breeze moved the eucalyptus, scenting the air with the smell of a dry autumn. Three coeds were seated on a concrete bench, their profiles clean and hopeful in the fading sunlight.

Laura was idling a Volvo in the parking lot.

When she gave the horn a polite toot, Silver came running. He didn't know why he exerted himself so, except that he half wished the evening would end soon. He was confident that his memory would eventually return to the empty cells inside his head and he would have enough smarts to find out where the Greyhound bus ground to a halt and leaked puddles of oil, radiator fluid, and immigrants toting cardboard suitcases. In California, if your ride was the soles of your shoes or public transportation, you were truly low-income.

When he got in, Laura gave him a playful smooch on his cheek.

"Now wipe yourself," she said, smiling. Her own tongue swabbed the lipstick off her front teeth. "And duck your head."

Silver clawed at his cheek and reviewed his fingertips: lipstick the color of anemic blood. He lowered himself so as not to be seen, Laura all along petting the back of his head like a dog's. In fact, he whimpered once when she absently touched the wound on the top of his head.

When the Volvo pulled out of the parking lot and was finally speeding along, Laura told him he could sit up again. He obeyed, the collar of his shirt whipping in the wind of a half-open window. He was blinking at the strange sight of a college situated in a clean residential area when he experienced another jolt of recalled memory. He had seen such places on television but never believed that they existed, house upon house in which the lawns were mowed, leaves raked, and chubby-kneed children played patty-cake. In these older established home fronts, grandfatherly figures smoked pipes while clipping hedges with well-oiled clippers.

Laura stuck in a cassette of religious music, a choral group.

Silver conjured up in his mind a group in satin robes perched on the high-priced real estate of a heavenly cloud. He pictured himself falling through the floorboards of a cloud, for he suspected that he was weighed down with the seven deadly sins, and then some. He winced when the group's voice went up on, "O, Sinners shall ye stop your ways, or be crunched."

What rhythm!

They drove in silence into a lush residential area. The homes were well ordered, segregated by wealth and class from the hodgepodge barrio dwellings of Los Angeles. The cars were new, the garden hoses were rolled up, and a knot of children played a game of hopscotch. The glow inside the Leave It to Beaver homes was welcoming. Something must have worked nicely in the childhood of these owners. They lived by the golden rule. Their hair was golden, their bank accounts golden. When they peed, more gold came out of them. And what the hell was that! Silver turned and strained his neck when he spotted on a lawn a cast-iron statue of a red-lipped Negro boy holding up a boot. Silver wondered, aren't those things outlawed? Any second he might hear the whip of a Confederate flag hoisted in the true-blue American sky.

"Oh, Jesus," Silver muttered, hands pressed between his thighs, a little shiver blossoming along his arms.

"You like Christian music?" Laura was pulling to the curb, composting leaves and twigs under the tires of her heavy Volvo.

"Yeah, I love it, especially what you got on." What a fat lie! He reminded himself to be careful what he said to the woman at his side. He noticed that her hands on the steering wheel had stopped their rhythm of tapping to the music. Where the rhythm was, he couldn't guess.

"Give me your face," Laura asked.

She was a demanding woman, all business, her fingernails lacquered and her hairdo, now straightened, cathedral high.

"Here, you hot tamale, my radical Chicano!" she barked, lips slowing budding into a wet pucker. She gave him a loud smooch and ordered, "Wipe yourself."

He sourly imagined himself unbuckling his pants and

lowering his underwear to clean himself with a bouquet of scented toilet paper.

She told him to get out and walk half a block. "You remember where the house is?"

Silver told her, no, he didn't remember.

When she pointed and started to explain, Silver stopped her by placing a hand on her beefy forearm. He could see the house. Wasn't it the one with a cross attached to the roof like a TV antenna?

Silver climbed out of the Volvo and watched it pull away, dragging with it a few migratory leaves. Standing alone on the curb, he feared that the homeowners in the neighborhood might part their curtains, peer out, and call the police on him. The moment became somber for him. Earlier, on the way over, he considered wheeling around and hightailing it out of Laura's life, abandoning altogether his position of Professor Something-Or-Other. But as he appraised the richness of the neighborhood, he judged that he was being too hasty, for after all, he was thirsty and hungry. Didn't Jesus say something about satisfying both?

He counted to ten before proceeding in a slow march to the house, the cross looming larger and larger over the spindly figure of his shadow. Yet, the cross had no moral effect on Silver, other than his wonderment at how an iron thing of that size stayed up in a strong wind.

He hesitated at the threshold of the house, swiping carefully the bottoms of his huaraches on a mat that read "Jesus Loves You." It seemed sacrilege to wipe the road's dust on such a message. Yet, he serviced the soles of his huaraches and entered without knocking because the front door was parted, a welcoming sign for latecomers. Immediately a parrot hollered, "Hello! Hello! Hello!" However, Silver didn't have much to say to the bird, especially after it squirted a stream of cement-colored shit in his presence. The parrot gazed down at its handiwork and quipped, "Good boy! Good boy!"

Laughter rose in what he figured was the dining room. He risked a few gingerly steps into a living room that resembled the waiting room of a mortuary. The couches and chairs were plain, the shag carpet recently combed—a couple of sets of shoe prints were visible. On the walls hung sea landscapes and— good god!—a portrait of Ronald Reagan. The light from the lamps was dim. A jar of multicolored jellybeans was centered on a coffee table. Silver marveled at the tire tracks from the bottoms of his huaraches that cut gullies in the deep shag.

"Hello, Professor Mendez," a voice greeted.

For a second, Silver believed the welcome belonged to the linguist parrot. But he was wrong. He was facing a smallish man in oversized glasses that were fashionable in the '70s; his pupils were two nearly transparent fish swimming behind the thick lenses. He wore a blue blazer, blue pants, blue tie. His shirt, though, was white, loose around the neck. Two necks might fit into the collar and still provide breathing room for a third neck.

"President Skaggs?" Silver braved. Not an hour ago his wife—Laura—was riding his meager body, his pants around his ankles, his Brown Power belt buckle chiming like a cowbell against the floor as she rode 'em cowboy. Presently Silver was extending his hand in greeting. He worried whether his hand gave off the aroma of Laura at near ecstasy. Would President Skaggs recognize her scent on his throat and pick up, say, the lamp and create another gash on his head?

"Wesley," President Skaggs corrected as he patted Silver's

shoulder warmly. "Have you started?"

Started?

Silver had indeed started something that employed two of his most alert senses, touch and taste. Was he referring to these senses?

"The school poem?" President Skaggs chuckled. He told him that they would talk about it later and patted Silver's shoulder a second time. "It's so good to have you on the faculty even if it's for only this semester." He waved a hand toward the dining room. "Come, let's eat something before the game."

That was the third time Silver had heard the word "game."

President Skaggs caught the lost look in Silver's expression. "We're playing the Lutheran Demons and they have a mighty strong defense."

Lutheran Demons?

"Division four. Religious schools." The president stirred his iced tea with a plastic straw, the dismantled glacier of ice cubes clinking. "You poets are not too keen on sports. You're in your lofty ivory tower."

Ivory tower? Was that what East Oakland was?

"No, sir, I'm just a regular guy," Silver protested.

President Skaggs chuckled and prodded Silver into the dining room where men in blue suits were huddled around a spread of finger food. Truthfully, Silver could use a drink—a beer, a shot of Tequila, and even the blush wine that comes in a box that you could squeeze like an accordion when it's empty. But there were only pitchers of iced tea and pulpy lemonade. Considering his options, either would sate his thirst. His mouth had been salivating, but that wetness receded like a drought when Laura approached, two small paper plates in her paws. Her lipstick was smeared, but he had the inkling that it was from chowing, not the plungerlike action that involved his neck and the lower depths of his body.

"Silver!" she called.

Silver gulped. Was that a wink in her left eye, no, her right eye, no, winks flashing the Morse code of deceit out of both eyes? Was she that brazen?

"You know Laura, don't you?" President Skaggs asked.

"Sure thing," Silver answered. He pictured her breasts, moist from his succulent lapping. He pictured the big dipper of moles on her left cheek. And he couldn't forget her navel, presently dark but a possible outlet for a piece of costume jewelry.

With a giggle, Laura shoved a plate into Silver's hands. "Hope you have an appetite." She winked boldly at Silver and then winked, less boldly, at President Skaggs, who blushed and pulled at his loose collar, exposing skin red as a rooster's wattle. The ice cubes in his iced tea began to melt.

Silver appraised his goodies: crackers and cheese, plus— good god!—two radishes positioned naughtily around a Vienna sausage, with sprouts and a leakage of mayonnaise.

President Skaggs might have noticed the artful culinary display, except he had wheeled around when he heard his name called.

"That's right," President Skaggs said. He stepped toward the buffet table, where he set down his glass of iced tea on a coaster. "It's time that we say a little prayer for this evening's game."

There it was again—"the game."

"Ladies, gentlemen, colleagues and students," President Skaggs called as he rang a spoon against the pitcher of lemonade. He lifted the twiggy nests of his eyebrows at two

students stuffing themselves with pups-in-a-bun. He waited
appropriately for them to swallow what was gorged in their
cheeks before he commenced. "Let's come together, Baptists
and non-Baptists, you few Lutherans."

The room came alive with laughter, but became quiet as
a funeral party when President Skaggs deepened his brow
with the ancient lines of a pious Christian. He chewed his
administratively tired lower lip.

Silver bowed his head, eyes on the plate that Laura had
prepared for him. He lacked an elementary study of Protestant
sects, but had the feeling that Baptists were probably very
conservative, the husbands and wives doing it with their
pajamas on—with the lights out, with the mirrors facing the
wall, the married Baptists would open the portals around
their genitals for a weekly exercise of pushpush. However, as
he tapped the Vienna sausage around on his plate and rearranged
the bean sprouts so that the mayonnaise was hidden, Silver
was convinced this was not true. He just had to recall Laura.
They were nasty as everyone else.

"Lord, take care of our youth today, our team," President
Skaggs prayed loudly. "Be sure that they beat the Lutheran
Demons, that we the Baptist Saviors improve our pre-season
record to two and two. But in your eyes let us win fairly.
Grace our school with a better record, that all may learn
from it." President Skaggs also mentioned those who were
too ill to join the evening, especially Paul Baker, a generous
soul who funded Baker Hall and Baker Gymnasium, and
whose grandson attended the college.

When the prayer was over, Silver waited an appropriate
three seconds before he tossed the Vienna sausage into his
chops, thus destroying Laura's prank.

★

The gymnasium was larger than any of the three main buildings that made up the campus. Cheers echoed off the ceiling, cheers and the blare of the marching band presently seated but, feet tapping, ready to swagger into formation. At that moment, the cheerleaders populated the floor, along with two students with industrial dust mops. The pep squad led a religious anthem sung by the five hundred or so souls who pounded their shoes each time a cheerleader, all smiles, was thrown into the air, the parachute of her tiny skirt flaring and, thus, slowing her descent.

Silver squeezed himself into a seat next to a man he didn't know or wish to know: his droopy collar was adorned with a soggy clip-on bow tie. The man sported a crew cut, a tweed coat with a college pin in the lapel. And was that a calculator on his belt?

"Your first game?" the man inquired.

"Yeah, which one are we?"

The man appeared puzzled. "You're not a sporting man, are you?"

The nerve, Silver fumed. The pinhead looked like he might break a sweat gripping a mechanical pencil. And to pick up a salad fork, the dude might need two hands and a male girdle wrapped around his middle to keep from suffering a hernia. What was he talking about? Silver had pushed shopping carts loaded with bottles and buckled tin, and he and a buddy had once carried the shell of a burnt-out Volkswagen all the way to the junkyard and then carried it back when the junkman belittled them by saying that it wasn't worth more than five dollars for scrap metal. Still, Silver remained polite. "Nah, not since I got thrown out of a Raider's game."

Silver smiled triumphantly. He was experiencing a rehabilitation of his memory, dark and embarrassing as it was. He recalled being thrown out of the game for not having purchased a ticket (true), being drunk to the point of crawling (also true), and copping a feel (real true) from a woman he assumed in his drooling stupor to be his girlfriend but later discovered was an usherette with a powerful punch. How the Raiders were bloodied that day and, in the fashion of a loser, he too!

"Our team," the man pointed out, "is over there. In red and white." The pinhead, a friendly fellow, chuckled. "By the way, I'm Theodore Scambray. I teach in the nursing program."

Nursing program?

An egghead, Silver surmised from the bow tie, the white shirt, and the white socks revealed below his high-water plaid slacks. However, as much as he regarded the guy as a nerd, he debated whether to ask his opinion about the wound on top of his head. Earlier, when he used the bathroom at the president's house, he parted his hair and audited the outer limits of his unfortunate wound, traced it gingerly, for Silver was allergic to pain. He probed his boo-boo, as his mother called such a gash, with a washed hand and Q-tip drawn from a box in the medicine cabinet. He noted, in his unscientific way, its redness and wondered whether a swig of alcohol in its tiny mouthlike gap might help heal it—or, at least, give it a little bit of a buzz. Silver was concerned about infection. Perhaps he might come down with lockjaw or, who knows, a snowy season of dandruff. After all, he would have to refrain from washing his scalp for a couple of days.

Suddenly, the band assembled into squads and marched with precision to center court, the drums beating out a rhythm of—good god!—"Dixieland." A piccolo added to the tempo, and the band was off with a sea of fans on its feet, hands pressed to their hearts. And were those tears of patriotism in their eyes? Did they all come over on the Mayflower?

"Oh, Jesus," Silver moaned.

The man next to him shook a fist in the air. "That's the spirit!"

Silver chanced a relationship with the pinhead. "Hey, bud, can you look at this?" He lowered his head, pried apart the mop strings of his hair, and shared with this friend a close-up view of his scalp.

"When was the last time you shampooed your hair?" the pinhead asked.

Silver wasn't in the least insulted. He asked: "Why?"

"You've got to keep an injury like this clean." But the pinhead's attention swung from Silver's blood-flecked scalp to the inspiring sight of cheerleaders all in a line, their hips pushing alternately in one direction, then the other, each time the bass drum boomed. They fell out of formation and ran up the bleachers, swishing their pompoms and heart-shaped bottoms. Their short skirts fanned out. Their golden hair bounced and lashed wildly their perfectly upright shoulders.

"Oh, Jesus," Silver moaned a second time. He bowed his head, knuckle to his mouth. When he gazed up, his poetry student—Amber?—danced in the aisle, favoring him by swinging her left leg, then her right, in a little peek-a-boo that had Silver's jaw falling open.

"Professor Mendez!" she screamed.

"Hello," Silver managed, half rising to his feet, for he was a professor, after all, and should portend the stature and manners that fit his title.

"I wrote a poem today," she screamed, her breasts pushed out like a robin's, the elastic straps of her sports bra worked to the max. "It's called 'Memories.'"

Memories? If only he had his intact.

"I'll show you later," she promised.

No, she's showing me now, Silver reckoned, his eyes slicing away from her shapely legs, but not before taking in a sparkling anklet that spelled her name.

"You like it?" Amber caught Silver ogling her ankle. "My boyfriend gave it to me."

Silver swallowed. God, the lucky stiff.

Amber bounced away when a hoarse buzzer sounded.

Silver rose to his feet as the announcer announced the preseason match between the Lutheran Demons and the Baptist Saviors. He descended the bleachers and sought out President Skaggs, who, he discovered, was seated behind the bench of players. At his side was Laura, her fist jammed in a box of a Cracker Jacks.

"President Skaggs!" Silver called.

President Skaggs's eyes slowly swam away from the male cheerleaders assembling a human pyramid. The president's smile evaporated when he saw it was Silver. He was there for an evening of sports, not a faculty conference. What was this about?

"I have a headache," Silver yelled over the crowd.

President Skaggs hoisted a smile and hoisted up his pants. He couldn't hear over the din of sport mongers moving in and out of the bleachers. "You feel a poem coming on?"

"Nah, a headache. A typewriter fell on my head."

"What?"

"A typewriter hit me on my head." He touched his head

and screamed that he was in pain.

The cheers and foot stomps in the bleachers brought down a fine dust from the heavenly heights of the ceiling. The starting members of the Baptist Saviors basketball team zigzagged up court, the last of whom was the center, a monster with fur around his eyes, who dunked the ball ferociously.

"I use the computer myself." His eyes swam away from Silver in the direction of the school's team. He applauded when it was announced that the Saviors' center Lukas Romanov was, at 7'3", the tallest center in the conference.

Silver had to admit that he was in awe of the young athlete Romanov. He could have used that height earlier when he brought down the typewriter.

Laura responded quickly. "I'll take you home."

"No, I can go on my own." Silver had seen enough of Laura, of the college, of Simi Valley. His stomach was stoked on finger food and he had faith that he could move stealthily from bush to bush, tree to tree, parked car to parked car, and get out without the local police leveling a nightstick against his skull.

She whispered in her husband's ear, and he nodded his head as he produced car keys from his pocket.

"No, I can wait," Silver argued. In truth, he wanted to see Romanov score a couple of baskets and wouldn't have minded seeing the cheerleaders do the splits.

But Laura set down her box of Cracker Jacks on her folding chair. "You hot tamale," she cooed, but her suggestive title was drowned out by the farting blare of the tuba. Her claws in his forearm, she prodded him toward the door.

They returned to her house, and before he could tell Laura that he needed a drink, something stiff and a great quantity of it, Silver had his Hawaiian shirt ripped over his head and pants around his ankles. The parrot screamed behind his hooded cage, "Good boy! Good boy!"

"Do you think we should?" Silver asked. He pointed to the parrot's cage. "The little guy might tell on us." And who knows, the parrot might learn a string of dirty words that could be attributed to him.

"You hot Chicano tamale!" she screamed repeatedly as she ignored his worry. Her own blouse was off, but her bra remained intact. Her tall hairdo began to totter as she leaned over and moved the coffee table out of the way.

During this tryst, however, he had a nice pad of carpet to protect his back from her punishing demands for more. His lover, the wife of a president of a small Baptist college, left her hand prints in the carpet where for at least ten minutes she assumed a doggie-style posture. And bark she did, all the way to the finish line.

"Oh, that was A-OK," she moaned afterward, an unlit cigarette in her mouth. She sat up momentarily and then lay back down, seemingly exhausted. Her tall hairdo was off its lacquered foundation.

"Do you want me to get you some matches?" Silver asked. His pants were still around his ankles. His beard was splayed from smooching her pussy.

"Nah, just get the rake." She raised a limp arm and pointed to the hallway closet.

Sure enough, when he opened the closet door, he caught a short plastic rake as it fell out. He was mystified. He twirled it in his hands, but when Laura called out, "What's taking you?" he hurried back to find her settled on her back and savoring the afterglow of sex.

"Who do you think will win tonight?" Silver asked.

"Shut up," Laura sighed. Her hand was between her thighs and her middle finger started moving with the great speed of a stenographer.

Silver shrugged his shoulders and got busy, moving the rake across the shag carpet. He considered whistling as he worked but feared that the bird might join him. He lifted up both of Laura's legs to wipe away the handprints, evidence that naughtiness had occurred on a night that, thanks to the remarkable stature of Lukas Romanov, the Baptist Saviors would chalk up another win.

Chapter Four

Satisfied by a diligent combing of the shag carpet, Laura drove Silver to the house where he rented a room. In the idling Volvo, she patted the inside of his thigh and boasted, "I knew it was true about Hispanic Catholics—great uncircumcised lovers!" She planted a noisy kiss on his throat, bruised with the marks of powerful hickeys, and with a wiggle of her fingers shooed him out of her Volvo. She drove away with her eyes raised to the rearview mirror. To Silver, she had the look of a bandit. What she was stealing, he didn't know, but he found himself waving good-bye to something.

Silver surveyed the place where he had apparently rented a room. The house was white, bordered with flowers, shaded by an expansive elm, and—good god!—owner of the cast-iron statue of the red-lipped Negro boy he had seen earlier. Had he actually rented a room from such a person? What was wrong with him? He detected that he was only a block away from the Skaggs's residence. He tiptoed in belief that the additional height of two inches might provide him with a view of the cross mounted on their roof. If he could only boost himself up on the shoulders of Romanov. He could probably glimpse Laura's house and maybe Russia, too!

"Oh," he warbled like a pigeon, eyes raised beatifically skyward for a sign of god. But no god of any stripe appeared.

Silver could scope out behind the curtained front window an elderly woman knitting what appeared to be a cap or, on second glance, a coat for a rodent-sized dog. He approached the front door nervously, but didn't feel like wiping his feet on yet another mat that read "Jesus Loves You." Instead he turned around and made his way back to campus, trying his best at playing the role of a neighbor out for a walk to aid his digestion. However, he had to scoot inside the bushy branches of a privet hedge when a patrol car—*la chota*—cruised up the street looking for trouble. To Silver's mind, its sinister lights were eyeballing the gutters for poets and lowlifes. He fit both descriptions.

Inside, the hedge held abandoned birds' nests, candy wrappers, Frisbees, tennis balls, and shuttlecocks. Silver made out the sounds of breathing that nearly matched his own. He sniffed shallowly and winced at a vaguely familiar scent that reminded him of wet wool. When he peered deeper into the depths of the privet hedge, he confronted a freckle-mugged dog curled up on a pile of leaves. They eyed each other, not in the least upset by the other's presence. The dog sniffed the air about them and rolled his tongue over his lips, Silver aware that the dog was picking up the scent of Vienna sausages, that and the mighty smell of Laura's sex.

"Hey," Silver greeted.

The dog wagged his tail once and licked Silver's outstretched hand.

"Be cool, dog," Silver advised and jumped out of the shrub with leaves in his beard. "I'll check you out later."

Back on campus, he devised a bed on top of the table: his mattress was old student term papers, bubble wrap, and padded envelopes found in a drawer. Before he turned the light off, he studied the photos of the Petersen family, a healthy family unit. They probably had a vacation home on a lake and a boat to take them out to the center of the lake, where they spent mornings catching trout and hammering them dead with oars when they were spread out on the deck.

When the telephone rang, he pulled on his beard and fancied Laura in pajamas on the other end. He let it ring ten times before he picked up and said, "OK, Laura, four times in one night is all this *vato* can spare."

"Where is it?" the voice asked roughly.

"Where's what?"

"You like your fingers?"

Silver despised crank calls. Since the call was coming into a phone that was not his, thus not traceable, he let the quills of his anger perk up. He gave the person on the other end the finger. "Yeah, and I like my dick, too. In fact, I'm known in some circles as the hot Chicano tamale."

The voice on the other end gave his word of honor that he wasn't going to have either of them left unless he delivered. He chuckled and reported that the hot tamale thing might be pushed down his throat. The person then hung up.

Delivered?

Silver stood in the middle of the office, shaken by the call. No dick and no fingers? Let his nose fall from leprosy before such calamity should visit him. Hell, he could always wear a Band-Aid where his nostrils once ventilated smoggy air. He ran his hand through his beard pensively. A no-fingers and no-dick life was truly no life at all. To remedy his fear, to calm his flashpoint of misfiring nerves, he pulled down from the shelf an overweight anthology of English literature, rifled through the pages, and read a poem by John Keats lamenting death in a faraway bog in a faraway time. He climbed onto his rack of a bed, where, lips moving, he read until the inertia of boredom sagged open his chops. His eyelids became the weight of magnets, of mortality itself. He began to admire English majors throughout the country.

Poor kids. They had to read such stuff?

How did I get here? he asked himself as he nodded off. In his dreams, a shit-faced redneck from Kern County was hurling beer bottles at him. The dream was undecipherable, a mess of images. He was bothered by a herd of cows following him down a ravine. He came upon the wreckage of a plane crash and red ants hustling off the eyelashes of its dead pilot. He witnessed water gurgling from the dry earth and a coyote howling from a toothache. Silver kicked in his sleep and ground his teeth. He smacked his lips, but found no moisture. He was tormented by a squad of burning tumbleweeds rolling in his direction, followed by his mother squirting lighter fluid on them. The world was on fire, and the mother of all fires was coming his way. "I need a drink!" Silver screamed as he woke in a sweat, the firecracker of bubble wrap snapping under his weight. He could smell the stink of worry on his body for his memory had returned and he didn't care for what he could remember— a scolding mother took up room in almost every lit and unlit compartment of his brain cells. He was suddenly privy to his personal history and nearly opted for another typewriter falling on his head and wiping out his memory again, this time for good.

"Why me?" Silver cried.

Bitterly, he discovered he had been no good in school, no good on the playing field, no good in his choice of a career path. Girls stayed away, and bullies walked in his shadow. And right after high school, he took a job at a Jack-in-the Box, where on the night shift he tortured hamburger patties, chicken parts, and headless fish in hot oil. Then he attended Bakersfield State as a Chicano Studies major, but failed to earn a degree. He summed up his career: three books, two of which were staple jobs done in dirty kitchens, and another a university press book—this one, titled *Raza Moments*, was selected by a buddy for a literary prize a decade ago, a buddy who bartered, "If I choose you, I don't have to pay you the three hundred I owe you, right?" With such a back-room policy, he was published and made a minor splash among the few friends he had who could read.

Silver woke from that nightmare to face another nightmare, one that was real and potent. Wasn't he teaching at a Baptist college? Didn't he just go to bed with the president's wife? He scooted off the table, stretched, and slipped into his Hawaiian shirt that looked better on the chair he had draped it over than on his own body. A lance of sunlight thrust through the blinds. He raised the blinds and, pulling the cord of his beard, stood at the window. A few early-bird students were scratching about in a courtyard dark with early-morning shadows. Their breath hung in the air and disappeared quickly.

When he emerged from the office, Silver waved at a youth who greeted him with a Brown Power salute of a clenched fist and yelled, "*Hola*, Professor Mendez!" Was that the kid in his poetry class?

Silver located a men's room, where he washed his face and scrubbed his teeth with his fingertips. He second-guessed his instinct to gargle with the liquid soap; instead, he rinsed his mouth. He wiped his eyes with a damp paper towel, inspected the wound on top of his head, and used the toilet that offered hygienic paper yokes for the seat, a lovely experience that awed him when he flushed: the paper and all of what a few minutes before was a part of him was sucked powerfully away.

He washed again. After opening up his wallet—seven

one-dollar bills—he elected to search out the campus convenience store. He bought a toothbrush and toothpaste, an
investment that he believed necessary: he would hate to wilt
the relationship between him and Laura over a little bad
breath. Plus, he believed only in the most basic of hygiene.
Now, if only he could change his underwear.

From there, he located the gym, showered, and brushed his
teeth. He returned to the bookstore, where at the outdoor café
he splurged on a coffee and an onion bagel as heavy as a horse-
shoe. He blew on the coffee and sipped cautiously. He tore his
bagel in half and ate it slowly as he watched a few of the morning
students, all early risers, nondrinkers, nonfornicators, come and
go in clean and starched clothes. The morning was advancing
and the once-cool air had moved somewhere, possibly downward
to the roots of the lawn. The sun had risen over a line of
eucalyptus. Its light was in the faces of everyone on campus.
They were all smiles. He understood why when he glanced
at the campus paper, a weekly, flapping on the table and doing
its best to get his attention. The Baptist Saviors had crushed
the Lutheran Demons, 65–46. Sports were front-page news.

When Silver turned the page, he nearly spit out his bagel. He
was facing a photo of himself, and, for one delirious moment,
he thought it was a wanted poster. However, the caption
read: "Chicano Poet to Read His Hispanic Poetry." The news
article announced that the reading would take place in Baker's
Lounge in the commons at noon. Silver didn't require a watch
or a sundial to calculate that it was only a few hours before
noon. He rose to his feet, chugged his coffee, and galloped up
the steps with the bagel around his thumb. He was going to
get out of town—now!

But at the top of the landing, he was stopped by a woman

with her blouse buttoned all the way to her throat and the hem of her dress nearly dragging like a sack. Her hair was gray, her eyes gray. But she lifted a smile to Silver. Her teeth were gray, too.

"Professor Mendez," she greeted him brightly. Her hands were up on her breasts as if she were trying to hide them. "Your check is ready."

Check?

Silver threw her a puzzled look, and she caught it in her wide smiling face.

"We're so sorry you had to wait," she continued. Her face became small from embarrassment. "Two months without salary is hard on a person."

Two months? A laugher!

Silver had gone a whole year without a paycheck. What was a couple of unsalaried months in the life of a poet? Still, he fought the urge to rub his palms together, a lowly gesture that might shock this woman who, he noticed, resembled a missionary from an outpost in rural China. Moreover, he didn't have to be an accountant to understand that money was coming his way. "When can I pick it up?"

"Right after lunch."

"I can't do it now?"

"No, I have a meeting to go to." Her hands fell from her breasts, as if she were exposing herself. She had the appearance on her face of, "What do you think?"

"Where's your office?" Silver asked.

"Silly, you know where!" She winked at him, then reminded him that it was in Administration, second floor, room 2031. She also reminded him that President Skaggs would be at the poetry reading and hoped that he—Silver—would have the school poem finished. She winked, twisted around, and departed, her bottom wagging just for him—or so he imagined. He touched his furry chin in contemplation: Did I go to bed with her, too? If so, did she ask for it in missionary position? Or was she like Laura, a woman who liked it on top? He would have scratched his head for an answer, but he feared reopening the wound.

He returned to his office, where he futilely searched for his poetry book in the drawers and shelves. He chewed his fingernails as if the pink flesh beneath them held the answers. He then called Tyronne, his ex-roommate, in Oakland, bass player in two funk groups. "Come on, bro, be home."

A lazy voice on the other end said: "Yeah."

"Tyronne, it's me," Silver cried in a hurried voice. He was used to talking on pay phones where every second cost a pretty penny.

"Yeah," he repeated. His voice became even lazier, gooey syrup from an Aunt Jemima bottle. Then he barked, "Where are you, dawg?"

Silver could envision Tyronne sitting up on the couch, mad as hell at Silver for the rent he never paid. "Ty, I'm going to pay you."

"I don't take aluminum cans!"

Silver corrected his friend by telling him that he had a college job, that a paycheck was on its way. "I got to ask for a favor."

"You always asking! If it wasn't for the Korean boy who moved in, I'd be like you, man, out in the rain pushing a motherfuckin' shopping cart."

After Silver was booted out of the apartment, Tyronne took in an engineering student from Seoul, Korea. He had a full-ride scholarship, and money for him was no problem.

"Yeah, but I'm going to pay. Honest. My word is good as an IOU."

"IOU my—what your kind of people call it—*nalgas!* My big, black butt!"

They argued back and forth, Silver now more relaxed. Halfway through their debate about each other's laziness, he became aware that he was not on a pay phone at a greasy station but one that belonged to a college professor. Silver begged Tyronne to fax a few poems from his book, *Raza Moments*—a box of musty copies was in the hall closet— and gave him the number to the fax machine in the office. Silver begged Tyronne, and Tyronne said that he might oblige him after he watched Judge Judy at eleven. He hung up.

Silver didn't have time. From his office, he retraced his steps to the house where he rented the room. Before he arrived there, though, he took a peek into the privet hedge where he had encountered the dog, a companion doing hard time. He was still there, lips wet, Silver suspected, from bringing himself out of hiding to lick a moist lawn.

"I'll bring you something back," Silver promised.

The dog wagged its tail twice and lowered its head onto the tenderness of its dirty paws.

Silver avoided direct eye contact when he walked past the cast-iron statue. He pushed his hands into his pocket for the key with the key chain that said "Jesus Loves You," but pushed it back into his pocket when his landlady greeted him at the front door. She was gripping a single knitting needle. Silver, knees weak, faltered in his march: Is she going to drive it through me? But he recalled Rodney King, still bruised in mind and heart but who—as he mumbled through a swollen jaw for the press—took it like a man.

Silver was prepared to take a couple of stabs from an old lady with bluish hair. There didn't seem much strength in her. She was small, dressed in a plaid dress, and wore a single strand of pearls. A pin sparkled on her collar. When she smiled, a fan of wrinkles appeared around her eyes.

"You didn't come home last night," she said. Her face showed concern beneath a light powder of makeup. "I was worried."

Silver was touched. To play out that feeling, he touched his heart and felt its two-cycle action.

"I made a pie this morning," she said. "You like apple, don't you, Professor?"

The pipes inside his stomach and lower tract began to shimmy.

"Sorry I didn't call." Silver fibbed by telling her that he had been working on a poem all night. Perhaps it was true: he pictured naked Laura on all fours, an image that he might haul to a typewriter someday when he was an old horny toad and only the memory of their forbidden love would placate his lust.

They went inside together, the elderly landlady going first and Silver squinting and pulling on an ear as he searched his mind for her name. Margaret? Grace? Pearl, like her necklace? But his worry vanished as his nostrils flared to a breaking point. He picked up the smell of pie and coffee. His tongue became bathed in a hungry man's saliva.

"Smells good!" Silver caroled. Immediately, he admonished himself for boldly confessing his hunger. The bagel he had eaten had amounted to almost nothing but hard bread with a Jewish history. He needed the pick-me-up of Pilgrim sugar.

"The apples are from our tree." Her cheeks were apples, her hands the dough of soft living.

Silver spotted his reflection in her eyeglasses. He didn't resemble a professor but a gaunt coyote that lived on bugs, snails, and river weed. He was sickened by the shady appearance, and embarrassed. Still, he relinquished his assessment of himself and trailed his landlady into the house, the foyer, and through the living room, where he noted a Ronald Reagan portrait above the couch—was that new? The cozy surroundings all came back: the maple furniture, the shaggy carpet, the heavy lamps with bloomerlike shades, the family photos on the walls, and plastic plants whose leaves spilled from vases. On the couch were gathered balls of yarn. Next to the yarn rested a large-print Bible with its pages open. Silver could make out the chapter titled "Isaiah" and wondered what that prophet had done to get in such an important book. He pulled on his beard, but no wisdom came to him.

In the kitchen, more family photos adorned the walls. Silver nearly gasped when he slinked under yet another portrait of Ronald Reagan. The portrait was big as life, no, much bigger because no matter where Silver stepped Reagan's smiling eyes followed him.

"Please have a seat," the landlady said. She was rinsing her hands in the sink.

Silver pulled out a chair, but quickly cast a glance at the clock that read twenty to eleven, the meat grinder of time chewing up the morning. His attention was drawn to a small plastic bottle of prescription pills, he picked it up: Albert Bartlett. His ailment at the time? The Latin name of the pills was baffling.

"Mrs. Bartlett?" Silver called.

The apples on her face glowed. "You know better. It's Helen."

"I need something from my bedroom," Silver said.

"I washed and ironed your shirt."

Poor thing, Silver grieved. Perhaps she gagged when she unfolded his shirt and discovered to her horror a pair of dirty socks, sour smelling and mere nets where his big toe was jammed.

But first he ate his pie and drank his coffee, and repeated the activity when Mrs. Bartlett asked if he would like more. Mrs. Bartlett crowed how wonderful it was to have a man in the house. His chewing slowed as he recalled that her husband was dead. Of what, he was unable to remember and wasn't about to ask now that his throat was coated with sugar. Let them talk of nice things.

"Would you like me to do anything?" Silver volunteered. He was thinking of something like taking up his plate and coffee cup to the sink, but she said that it would be nice if he could remove a tree stump in the backyard. She glanced in the direction of a frilly curtain over the sink and laughed when Silver followed her gaze.

"Fooled you!" she taunted playfully. The apples on her cheeks reddened into a season of happiness, then paled. "Oh, my poor husband. He died not knowing who I was." Her cheerfulness vanished. She crushed and recrushed her paper napkin.

The two sat with their heads bowed. Silver counted the drips in the sink, rose, and took his plate and coffee cup to the sink, where he splashed them with water. He peered into the backyard, which was tidy, though the flowers had their heads bowed now that it was autumn. The wind had stripped most of the leaves off an apricot tree in the corner.

"Excuse me," he said. He walked slowly through the kitchen, Reagan's eyes crawling after him, and down the hallway. There were more family photos on the wall, plus portraits of George Bush and George W. Bush, the father/son tag team for corporate giants.

"Chumps!" Silver snarled.

Silver passed a bedroom with a door swung open and knew it belonged to Mrs. Bartlett by evidence of the mountains of yarn in a wicker chair. He journeyed past another bedroom converted into an office and, finally, he reached his bedroom, which was dark in spite of the white frilly curtains and a seascape of an old sailor, face lit with drink, painting a rowboat. The bed was maple, as were the chest of drawers, a rocker, a small table with a stack of *Reader's Digests* and another large-print Bible. He surveyed his surroundings and pondered, Now why am I here? A hush enveloped the room. A wind chime banged in the neighbor's yard. Then he remembered: I'm looking for my poetry book for the poetry reading! He rummaged through a small bookcase, and on his knees peered through the coffinlike darkness of under the bed. He couldn't locate a copy of his book, though he did salvage a ballpoint pen that read Regent Engineering. He wondered if it had belonged to Mrs. Bartlett's husband. Then he remembered the pills on the kitchen table. Silver wasn't up to date on medicine, other than aspirin and the mentholatum that he smeared on his chest in winter, but was familiar with forgetful retirees from his work in a library. He smoothed the bed cover, stroked it as if it could get better. Was Mr. Bartlett one of them during his life?

"Oh, no," Silver cried softly, his thumb absently clicking the pen. Her husband had died of Alzheimer's in the very room where he currently slept.

Chapter Five

Dressed in a fresh shirt, socks, and underwear, Silver returned to campus, stopping once at the privet hedge to ply the pooch with turkey lunch meat snagged from the refrigerator, and another time to pretend to tie his shoes—though he was wearing huaraches—when the police cruiser he had seen earlier crept by. Not him again! Silver hadn't lost so much memory that he couldn't size up the danger posed by police officers with free time on their hands. Munching the remains of his low-cal lunch off his mustache, the officer behind the wheel evaluated what he might have presumed was riffraff, then drove away.

At his office, Silver joyfully discovered that Tyronne had faxed five poems.

"My bro!" He clenched his fist and made a mental promise to send his former roommate a money order when he picked up his check later in the day. But when Silver appraised the poems, he was startled at how many lines employed the words "fuck" or "shit" and "eat my shorts, white America." His angry attitude was unsophisticated but true right down to his bone, particularly during those unfortunate moments when he raced and missed a public bus by thirty feet, black exhaust whirling in his face—everyone had a car and car payments except him and the unwanted. Still, Silver registered in his mind that the tone of his poems was inappropriate at *this* college. They were poems intended for gatherings at open-mic cafes or late-night beer bashes, where in the wee morning the wee poets would pass out on couches, warm half-full beer cans posted between their equally warm thighs.

Shoulders slumped, Silver lowered himself into the chair but quickly raised those skimpy empires of flesh and cartilage as he was struck by the insight that he could doctor his guttersnipe in favor of a civil language. Granted, the interior of his personality would be lost, but what was that anyhow? Hell, he could hardly remember who he was.

He spun a glance to the clock on the wall: twenty to twelve. He bowed his head and covered his eyes with his hands: he saw a Technicolor Ronald Reagan in Western attire. Scared to action, Silver licked a pencil and replaced "love" for "fuck," "flowers" for "shit," and "let's praise the happy trout that liveth in rivers, America" for "eat my shorts, white America." Silver adjusted his previous view about writing: golly, revision does work! He whacked his thigh with his pencil and yelled at the lazy, *mota*-toking alter ego who lived rent free inside him, "Finally, you've learned!" He proceeded to frisk the desk drawer for a paper clip to add order to his just-assembled manuscript.

But he found more than a paper clip within the tray of junk professors attracted like magnets. He found a single pellet of marijuana seed the color of sagebrush; he raised it toward the overhead light and studied it, exercising his talent as a part-time botanist. He tossed the seed in his mouth and chomped: the taste was indeed of marijuana, possibly from Michoacan or— ah, yes, he was too hasty!—from the back roads of hillbilly Bolinas. Although he had placed the origin of the seed's birth, he wasn't presented the opportunity to ascertain why it was in the drawer, for the telephone began to holler for attention. He picked it up on the third ring and asked roughly, "Yeah?"

"Where is it?"

"Is this you again, asshole?" Silver snapped, quick to recognize the voice that had called him the day before. Peeved, he put to use some of the words he had removed from his poems on the caller, those and new phrasings that came to mind. Finally, he hung up and proceeded to ransack the drawer. He found two more seeds, which he popped into his mouth like breath mints. Then he tasted a white substance that he believed at first was chalk dust. It was bitter: cocaine. He blew on the substance; indeed, it clouded in the air like toot. Silver, a pharmacist of drug life, was still considering his findings when the telephone began to ring again.

"Asshole," he shouted at the telephone. He picked up the receiver and slammed it back down.

However, he quickly reminded himself that he was not involved with the prankster, that he could take off for Oakland once he got a few coins making music in his pocket. He exhaled and then breathed deeply the stale air that filled the office. He was going to be Zen about the haranguing caller. He was going to ignore the voice on the other end, though he was bewildered by the taste of marijuana that lingered in his mouth. His attention was drawn to the photograph of Petersen and his family. His eyes were clear, his smile genuine. Was the guy a doper? A pusher?

"Nah," Silver muttered in half-disbelief. He searched the drawer for more seed, for more cocaine. Finding none, he gripped his poems and left, stopping to ask a coed the whereabouts of Baker Lounge. He found the place after a few twists and turns and a stop at a drinking fountain to moisten his lips for an hour of poetry.

Seated in the front row was President Skaggs, his knees

daintily pressed together. In the corner, Laura was stirring pink lemonade—leftover brew from the rah-rah party from the night before? She abandoned her interest in the pitcher of lemonade in order to fiddle with a platter of carrots, radishes, quickly browning apple slices, and dicelike cubes of yellow and white cheeses. She gazed up from her handiwork, smiled. Silver could swear that she had floated him a kiss on the tips of her fingernails, though she could have been wiping her mouth with the back of her hand. He gulped and shivered, rattling the poems like a tambourine in his hands.

"President," Silver greeted.

"No, it's Wesley to you." President Skaggs rose, released a smile, and pumped Silver's hand two times. "Are you going to read the school poem?"

The school poem?

"I have a draft," Silver claimed. He recalled that the president had assigned him to compose a poem that celebrated—yes, this must be it—Christian kindness? He waved vaguely at the poems in his hand.

"Say, where did you get your sandals?" The president's attention had floated downward.

Hiking up his pants legs, Silver peered at his road-worn huaraches that had stepped over and between drunken poet friends, winos, and snowstorms of Big Mac wrappers in East Oakland. But where did he purchase them? He envisioned the immigrant mobs at a Saturday swap meet in Oakland. "Oh, I don't remember."

"Our Lord most likely wore sandals like yours."

"How clever of him." To Silver, his loose-lip comment reeked of stupidity and sounded like a downright wisecrack. Then he recalled the story behind his huaraches. But how could he tell President Skaggs that he had bartered for them by swapping two burrito-thick joints back in 1997? But that was years ago. While the joints were presumably gone, the sandals, with him in them, were still on the road.

When Silver heard the call of "Professor Mendez," he gazed up, momentarily lost in the fluorescent glare of the room, for he had swung his head with such swiftness that the blood in his brain had the force of a wave hitting the shore. Thus, the dizziness. Thus, his hand reaching to hold onto the front-row chair that President Skaggs had claimed. But he righted himself and nodded at the blue-blazer-wearing fellow who had bellowed his name.

"Are you almost ready?" the blue blazer asked. He was fiddling with papers in his open briefcase. He held up a hand, fingers splayed: five minutes, then you start, was the signal.

"*Simón!*" cried Silver, fist clenched.

In spite of his apparent bravado, Silver was sinking in spirit and could have used the sugar rush of a glazed donut. He began nervously to observe the students with backpacks on their shoulders bumping into the room. They're getting extra credit for showing up, Silver wagered. When he had done readings in the past, only people in need of a warm place to sit for an hour or two came to hear him, those and perhaps friends to whom he owed money. But he didn't owe this crowd any money, or not that he knew of. This crowd was full of clean-cut remnants of the 1950s, the young men in white shirts and pressed slacks and the young women in skirts that hid dimpled knees. Everyone except what's-his-name, the young man who had come into his office with his poem. The young man with lances, shiny chrome balls, and doodads in his face took the chair next to the president.

"Hello, Jason," President Skaggs greeted. He hoisted a smile as he crossed his legs in the direction of Jason.

The young man muttered, "Yeah."

"That's a mighty long skateboard," the president tooted.

"Yeah," he answered. His front teeth proceeded to bite his lower lip, a cannibalizing action that had the chrome ball on his chin disappearing, then reappearing with the shine of spittle.

"How's it going?" Silver crowed to the youth. Secretly, he had the urge to put a boot up the young man's butt and scold, "Grow up!"

"Yeah, how's it going, Jason?" jollily asked President Skaggs.

Jason snarled. "Uncle, Professor Mendez said it's OK to choke a doobie before we write."

Silver flushed. He let the poems in his hands flutter to the carpeted floor as he considered the scaredy-cat option of scampering from the room. Uncle? Choke a doobie? Moisture surfaced from some shallow spring in his armpits. His hair became an Everglades of sweat in which dandruff floated and would soon wash down the side of his face. Choke a doobie? He bent down and gathered the poems.

The president, however, couldn't make sense of Jason's meaning.

"Wesley, you know, I guess we better get the show on the road." Silver stepped backward toward the podium, distancing himself from Jason, and was greeted by Laura, who presented him with two glasses of lemonade, each at breast level and perhaps as sour as her personal tankers.

"I'm washed," she whispered.

Washed?

He accepted refreshments and set them carefully on the

podium, but immediately picked up one because his tongue required a bath of that citric concoction. With the glass to his mouth, he sized up the crowd of young people. Where did they come from? All tidy and brushed, none of them with tattoos or purplish hair. Silver began to wonder whether he had somehow missed a fashion trend, a change from jeans punched out at the knees, loose T-shirts, and engineer boots with chain anklets. Back in the 1970s, he had missed a trend toward employment, he the last Chicano poet out on the streets when the party was long over. Was he so absent-minded that he didn't catch on that Old Spice cologne, parted hair, and tucked-in shirts had returned?

His debate ended when the man in the blue blazer, the one who beckoned him earlier, approached Silver. Silver vaguely remembered him, something about a faculty meeting, or had they at one time stood at urinals together talking shop? Yes, Silver recalled, they had met at the former, at a meeting where Silver had the Herculean strength to stifle a yawn that would have let on that he didn't belong in academia.

"We're so glad that you can do this for us," the blue blazer said. His scalp showed through his thin hair. Veins on his nose showed, too. The foliage of hair engulfed his ears.

Silver harbored a thought: this brother is a solitary boozer.

The blue blazer brought from his coat pocket a Post-It. He swung his reading glasses to his face.

That's my life? Silver asked of himself. My accomplishments on a Post-It with a backside sticky as snot?

But Silver was wrong once again. On the Post-It the blue blazer announced other campus activities, including the bible study group at four, the cleanup crew for the up-and-coming basketball game against Loyola Marymount, and the blood drive to be held in the gymnasium on Saturday. His own intro was simply, "Let me proudly introduce Hispanic poet Silver Mendez." The blue blazer vacated his brief reign at the podium with the Post-It stuck absently to the sleeve of his coat.

The roomful of Baptists began to applaud. Their souls were stirred by the appearance of a man in sandals and a long beard. Little did they know that, like Christ, Silver fasted, was wanted by the law, had been punched and kicked, and more than once slept with his head on a rock while crickets buzzed in his ears. And, like Christ, he prayed for salvation, mainly his own but also for kicked dogs and the truly derelict.

"Thank you, brothers and sisters." He thanked the blue blazer, President Skaggs, the staff, and his own students. "The first poem I'm going to read is . . ." Silver looked down at the poem titled "In Your Face, You Piece of Shit," which he had retitled properly "In Your Sweet Place," a sweet choice, for he spotted Jason, the skateboarder, throwing back a few M & Ms. He next scanned the poem for cuss words, political rhetoric, and the emission of bodily liquids, but found none. He cleared his throat, swayed left, then right, as he got into a Chicano poet groove. He stopped his swaying, although his beard continued to swing like a pendulum. He boomed the poem about riding the BART train late at night. He boomed how the seats were ripped just like—good god, he saw it coming!—like the speaker in the poem. The speaker, a staggering figure, had consumed an overpriced pissy beer at a Raiders exhibition game. But he quickly changed the Raiders game to a jamboree of white-shirted Promise Keepers and the refrain, "Drunk on the spirits of human love." Now sweat poured like liquor from under his arms.

President Skaggs applauded.

Laura, still stationed by the platter of food, fit a carrot into her mouth and chomped heartily.

In the imitation of speed, he next screamed a poem about a friend who fell asleep on his Harley doing 75 on Highway 880. He next read a sonnet about a cockroach rowing his dirty little legs in a bowl of *menudo*—he stopped in the second stanza to explain *menudo* and its medicinal power of cutting the edge of a *cruda*, a hangover, a word that brought a frown on the president's face.

Silver tried to correct his error. "You know the guy I just talked about?"

Blank faces.

"The guy who fell asleep on his motorcycle?"

A few nodded their head.

"He was tanked on Night Train, the worst kind of brew you can bring to your lips, though in my time Thunderbird used to really get you so ripped you pee your pants. You know what I mean?"

When the president activated the frown that lived beneath his jowls, Silver admonished himself for bringing up the subject of drink. He emitted laughter. "Just joking with you." He looked down and scratched his nose at the next poem titled "Crowley's Crawl." When did he write that? He stammered through the poem, feeling rightly that he was not reaching his audience, or himself for that matter. The poem was a puzzlement of past and present tenses, of bad spelling and grammar, and even of incorrect geography—how in the world the Amazon flowed through the Congo was anyone's guess. His mind, however, lit up as he judged the poem as an imitation of drunkenness and may have been written, Silver realized, in such a state. He sensed the crowd's confusion and to lasso them back into the moment, he deserted the theme of the poem and ended by adding a non sequitur, "Drunk on the spirit of human love."

The Baptists applauded.

Silver caught on. He heralded two more poems, adding that phrase and other phrases that resounded a quasi-biblical message, all the while supposing that he had a rebirth as a religious poet and was, yes, a poet like Kahlil Gibran, except Christian. He beamed at the audience. He didn't feel in the least like a charlatan when he called out "Peace and Love," but kept his hands at his side because he wasn't certain whether the peace sign was a pagan symbol or not. Why take a chance?

He then rifled through the faxed pages and winced at a note messy as graffiti in the corner of one poem. The communication was from Tyronne: "Your momma called and axed if you sold the hedge clippers for some brew 'cause she can't find 'em. Says you ain't going to get no mo' Christmas presents 'cause you lazier than a dead dog." Silver was furious at such an accusation, especially on the occasion of his apparent comeback as a poet. But the fury dissipated. After all, weren't a few students sitting on the edge of their chairs? Certainly that meant something.

But Silver sized up his mother's meanness and would answer her directly about the hedge clippers. No, he hadn't sold them. He had lent them to a buddy and, as he stood in front of the crowd, was mightily proud of his actions—this bud had just gotten out of a re-hab clinic in Vallejo and was going door-to-door seeking work as a gardener. No, Silver resolved to simmer down, to become Chicano Zen in his approach to mothers and other mean people. He stroked his beard, which zapped his fingertips with a charge of electricity.

The audience roared "Wow" when they witnessed the zap of electricity lift not only his beard but also a mighty wave of his hair.

"Yeah, man," Silver giggled. "Wow's *la palabra.*" While not a scientist, Silver deduced that his huaraches had picked up static from the blue carpet. Then, he mused over the possibility that God was talking to him, albeit through an assault of electrons.

"Did you see that?" he asked the audience after he patted down his beard and hair.

"Do it again?" cried a student from the back row.

The president turned and scowled at the student.

Silver was almost inclined to pull on his beard and repeat the sensation. But he thought better of it. Hell, he might re-create this noontime miracle and, then again, he might pull and pull and only get a scattering of loose hair. He couldn't risk disappointing the audience. Also, the blast of static hurt!

He asked the crowd for a question, for he had run out of poems to read.

Jason uncrossed his legs and asked, "You get high when you write? Is that why you got lightning out of your beard?"

President Skaggs sat up, his puny eyes becoming large behind his thick, oversized glasses. "What did you ask?"

Jason shrank, but not much. "Nothing." He spun a wheel on his skateboard, the ball bearings clattering like a roulette wheel.

"I think I heard you say 'high.'" His face darkened with wrath. "I don't know much about drugs, but I do know the meaning of 'high.'"

Silver rushed his lemonade down his throat, ice and all. His underarms were dripping like faucets. He was in a tight space, he, the poet who minutes ago was enjoying his new tenure as a religious poet, a Chicano Dalai Lama? Now he was being defrocked by a punk kid asking if he smoked *mota*. Of course he did! When he could get the good stuff, that is.

Skateboard under his arm, Jason got up and stomped out, the choker chain on his boots chiming the angry sound of Fuck You.

The crowd followed Jason's departure, which was followed by the president's departure, his steps nearly as quick as the young man's.

"Let's see," Silver began again, convinced that he had to get out of town post haste, on the back of a burro if need be. He could see why he had taken the job: money. Shit, now it appeared that he would have to spend a portion of it buying his mother a pair of hedge clippers. That purchase would have to wait, though. He was on thin ice, and he was chewing more ice when he brought the second glass of lemonade to his face. He then clapped his hands as his attention swiveled toward the display of food in the corner. "The poetry's over. It's a free-for-all for those carrot sticks."

★

Silver was ambushed by a delighted faculty, most of whom were dressed in blue blazers, including the female faculty and nine-to-five administrators. Two of the faculty members apologized for Jason's outburst and others frowned in agreement. It was clear to Silver that the sentiment was something like one bad apple of a student was ruining it for all the good apples. He felt safe among them.

"If it wasn't for his grandfather . . ." one faculty member commented mysteriously.

Two shushed him.

Silver lifted his eyebrows. This action puckered his forehead.

Still, no loose-lipped colleague tattletaled. They chewed the insides of their cheeks and jiggled the coins in their pockets. There was great interest when a pager began to buzz in one fellow's breast pocket.

Laura brought him a plate of carrots and apple slices, the fodder a horse might have enjoyed after a trot around a dusty ring. He accepted the plate, but avoided her gaze, which he could feel latched onto his throat.

"That was super nice," Laura remarked. "Let me pull your beard?" She winked boldly at him and slapped his arm playfully.

Silver had to turn and thank her. He had to admit that she was lovely in face, though large in body and the wife of someone else. "Thank you, Mrs. Skaggs."

She scowled and set a hand onto her hip—in profile, she looked like a teapot. "Get off it, buddy boy! You know I'm Laura."

Silver averted a scene by manufacturing a simple smile. He thanked everyone and hurried away, his poems rolled up and sticking out of his back pocket like a tail. But at the door he was lassoed by the woman who had earlier promised his paycheck. There was a naughty glint in her eye. "I have it for you," she quipped, her hand tucked under her sweater.

Have it for me?

The woman, who came up to Silver's shoulder, led him down the hallway. Silver braked at the drinking fountain and, after he sucked in a mouthful of chilled water, she pulled him away.

Soon, they were out in the courtyard, their shadows mingling in front of them on the cement walk. The air was scented with flowers past their prime and a fountain gargled seemingly clean water. The sun was coin-bright, and the sky was almost blue—the Santa Ana winds had whipped airborne trash and smog into San Bernardino County. Silver didn't require a clear day to view an argument between President Skaggs, the cuckolded husband, and Jason, his misbehaving student. Jason was stationed on his skateboard, his mouth busily chewing on M & Ms. President Skaggs was lecturing the youth none too softly. In fact, Silver thought he heard "shit" but it could have been "sheet," seeing how the wind fooled with the vowels once they left one's mouth.

"What's with those two?" he asked the woman.

The woman peered. "Oh, that's Mr. Baker's grandson. He's a spoiled boy who needs a man's paddling."

Silver caught the drift. The ol' granddad had helped build the present campus and the snotty kid imagined that he could do as he pleased. After all, he was a Baker, and a Baker was a good name to have if half the buildings on campus carried its name. The kid threw another handful of M & Ms into his mouth and rocked back and forth on his skateboard.

Silver sensed a hand on his waist.

"Silver," the woman whispered. From under her sweater, she brought out an envelope.

My paycheck at last, Silver guessed. What he had done for it he couldn't say, except lose his marbles from the typewriter incident. But the envelope that contained the check floated in his direction and then floated away. A game of tease.

"Are you going to see me?"

"See you?" Silver asked. Was he bedding down with two Baptist women? He closed his eyes briefly, but no matter how he tried, he couldn't recall any transgressions, doggie-style or otherwise, with the woman in front of him.

"Silver, don't play with an old woman's heart." She touched her heart when she made this remark. She reddened when she became aware that a button in the middle of her white blouse was undone.

To Silver, she suddenly turned into an old biddy. Fissures appeared around her mouth and her hands were peppered with age. The skin under her throat sagged like a pelican's and even the roots of her hair could not escape the frost of old age. He blurted out, "Well, how old are you?"

Her eyes filled quickly and leaked. She pushed the envelope at him and stomped away, yanking the hem of her sweater. Her dramatic act had briefly stopped the exchange between President Skaggs and Jason. She turned and yelled, "You don't like my poetry, do you? You lied to me!"

Her poetry?

Then he remembered. She had given him a folder some time ago. He had read them until he yawned and a flood of tears blinded him. He shrugged when she scolded him for being insensitive to lady poetry. As he started his rush off campus, he tore open the envelope that contained his check.

"Wow!" He stopped in his tracks, and not from another blast of electricity from his awe-inspiring beard, but from the check of $2,737.11. He nearly genuflected and praised the lord, and would have except he was a believer in private prayer, plus he didn't want to dimple his knees with grass stains.

Chapter Six

In a strip mall not far from the college, Silver found a grimy pay phone and searched the telephone directory for a check-cashing service, but discovered to his anger that the "c" pages were ripped out. He then searched for a bail bondsman, though he presently was not in need of one. He figured that catty-corner to the bail bondsmen would be an establishment that cashed checks, anyone's check, government or private, even those that didn't belong to you. Not in the least discouraged by the missing pages, he thumbed backward the short trip to the Bs—in his own troubled past, Silver was familiar with how the bail bondsmen worked in cahoots with the cash-checking services. Silver had frequented such places, where cashiers chewed gum behind plate glass and cameras were aimed on you like guns.

He tapped a finger against the ad: Honest Injun Larry Will Bail You Out. The white man in the ad sported an Indian headdress. In one hand was a bundle of greenbacks and, in the other, a tomahawk.

"Jesus," Silver moaned. "What place is this?"

Silver scribbled the address in red ink on his palm and pitched the telephone directory aside, the chain catching its drop like a noose. The directory bounced once, then swung until its heaviness settled it into place.

Silver looked left, then right. He asked himself, Where's the poor part of town? While no real estate agent, Silver did his math. He reasoned that most of the homes of Blanche were valued at a half-million, even the dinky ones with aluminum carports. People had jobs, people had savings. The homeless were nonexistent. The city, he also reckoned, hardly spent a dime for upkeep of its two parks since its citizens were prosperous and seldom ventured into the city parks. They preferred their own backyards. Sure, a city gardener planted petunias and hosed off the walks occasionally, but the city didn't have to police the parks for the homeless—or poets with their best lines etched in their foreheads—drinking from paper bags. He held the belief that the dogs in this neighborhood had been diligent students in behavioral classes, for he had seen two sporting ascots and barking with a clipped British accent. And the neighborhood cats? He suspected that those shiny and regularly de-wormed creatures were in magazine and commercial ads. They had it made in the shade.

Where were the poor immigrants? he was prompted to wonder, the ones who weekly bought fistfuls of lottery tickets? The answer lay at his feet; he noticed that the sidewalk dipped, ever so slightly, southward. He was more than certain when, across the street, he surveyed a rivulet of water flowing south—the automated sprinklers of the rich had kicked on and stayed on. Thus the sun-lit water flowed downward to remind the poor that the rich got to waste what was theirs. Silver, knees buckling, tottered as he was suddenly struck with poetry: he saw how the rich let water flow freely so that the immigrant poor—the gardener, the maid, the maid's children—would muddy their shoes and leave prints so that the authorities would always know their whereabouts. Silver shielded his eyes with a hand and envisioned *la migra* gathering them up for a quick trip to the border.

"Damn!" Silver admonished himself for not having a

single sheet of paper on which to write his impressions.

But for Silver, poetry had its time and place, and although the muse was calling him, he had to ignore the babe. His college paycheck required immediate cashing. Without real money—the hundreds, the twenties, the tens, all stinking of hard work—how could he board a Greyhound bus and ride away in style? He began his trek toward the main street of Blanche, now and then peering at the address on his palm. True to his instincts, he entered a neighborhood where the houses became less tidy, the parked cars older, and the dogs increasingly angry about something or other behind their chain-link fences. And was that the jingle of a radio commercial in Spanish behind a rickety fence? Was that the homey aroma of *frijoles* in the wind? But as quickly as the homes had become the affordable abodes for the regular Josés and Marías of the working world they became once again exclusive—Silver perceived the street's subtle climb. Had he gone through the poor part of town? Was that it? Two blocks of so-so housing?

He beckoned a boy on a bicycle to ask for the address, but the junior cyclist with parted yellow hair became scared, no, just mean, when Silver raised and presented the youth a red-inked palm. Silver asked, "Hey, Bart Simpson, you know where this place is?" The boy did a wheelie and rode away, screaming, "Bite me, pervert!"

"Now what?" Alarmed by the encounter, Silver ran to put distance between him and the boy. He ran until his lungs were stoked with fire and his beard dripped sweat that cascaded from his brow. His shirt clung to his back. The soles of his feet stung from the punishing slap of his huaraches. Head down, the spongy sockets of his lungs rasping for air, he rested at a curb and watched two ants between his feet struggling to lift a Popsicle stick. He was impressed by their strength and cooperation. The two stubborn ants rounded up two more ants, and, in the end, the gang of four was able to shoulder its treasure and stagger away.

"Right on, little brothers," he sang. It was a clear lesson for Silver, who felt he was better schooled by these bugs than any wiseass book, including—he gulped—his own out-of-print efforts. He almost became teary eyed when two additional ants volunteered their efforts. The burden for all six became light, the journey shorter, the reward tastier.

Refreshed from his repose on a curb, he rose stiffly and commanded his get-away sticks—his skinny legs with skull-like kneecaps—to march two blocks to a 7-Eleven for a Slurpee. He was glad for the cool air, though put off that there was so much to buy but no money to do the spending. He could have eaten a couple of bags of potato chips to replace his lost salts—he had sweated buckets.

He presented the clerk a soggy dollar, all the money he was willing to part with foolishly, and laid a hand on the girders of his ribs. His stomach called out for real sustenance—a Slim Jim sausage, barbecued pork rinds, Hostess Snow-Balls, or one of those burgers sunbathing under a heat lamp. Still, he had to save the few dollars he possessed. But before he left the store, he asked the clerk, a Pakistani with a beard that matched his own, for directions.

"Hey, you know Honest Injun Larry's?" Silver inquired after a quick slurp of his Slurpee. When he showed him the address on his sweaty palm, the clerk jumped back.

"Don't get blood on me, my friend," the clerk begged.

Silver threw him a confused look.

"Are you diseased?"

Silver fumed, but not righteously. He had been told to go away many a time, but seldom after a purchase, including a piddling one that amounted to ice, sugar, and blue dye. "I dropped some coins here, and you're calling me diseased?" Silver unruffled a snarl, though he was not in the least disturbed by the clerk's callous remark. But as a show of strength, he gripped his Slurpee drink until its paper container buckled.

"Your hand, my friend."

Silver examined his palm: the stigmata of red ink ran like blood. He was shocked himself, but wasn't about to let a sales clerk with a gut and the working pleasure of plying out twenties and tens all day get the better of him. In fact, he dismissed this merchant. The address was undecipher-able—was the one a nine, or was that nine really a one?

"You don't mind, do you?" Silver asked. He plucked a napkin near the dispenser on the counter and dabbed his palm; the address became a slur of pure red confusion. He walked out of the 7-Eleven, spotted a pay phone outside, and this time located within the bulky phone directory a check-cashing service called Magic Money. Not willing to recreate his last faux pas, he wrote the address on the inside of his wrist; he mumbled it three times and locked it inside his short-term memory. He slurped his ice drink and returned inside the convenience store, a chill riding his back because the yin-and-yang of hot and cold air was whacking out his body temperature.

"Hey, man!" Silver yelled.

The clerk sucked in a gut that hadn't experienced a single sit-up in years. His ring-endowed hands rested on the counter, but he withdrew them and settled them onto his hips, for he feared exposing his wealth. The clerk recovered his position: he was the boss of the place. He frowned.

"Where's Henry Street?" Silver pulled on the straw in his drink, now a sweet slush, until his cheeks collapsed.

"Your face is blue." The clerk pointed and stepped back, retreating from his previous position of boss.

"My face is blue, my hands are red. So what?" Silver was boiling a stew of anger in the pot of his soul. The clerk was getting on his nerves. But Silver realized that their business dealings—hadn't he bought a cold drink?—could turn to his advantage. He produced a chuckle; he parted his beard so that the clerk could see the good-natured intent of his teeth. "Hey, amigo, why don't you cash my check?"

The clerk shook his head.

"It's from the Baptist college. They're solid. Unlike you and me, they're going to a Christian heaven."

The clerk added a pout to his headshake.

Silver retracted his smile, his mouth lost in his wily beard. "OK, if that's the deal, then tell me where's Henry Street."

"I do not know the street." Headshake, pout, and shrug of shoulders.

Silver took it to another level. "Well, fuckhead, what do you know?"

When the clerk reached for the phone, Silver backed away from the counter and departed noiselessly. He had been in such a good mood since he finished his poetry reading and was handed his first paycheck. Now his personality was fouled by this encounter, a locomotive of dark anger running over the tracks of his pleated forehead. He had been considering going back to buy some goodies with his cashed check, but the movement of the clerk's hand for the telephone had changed all that. "You gotta work on your customer relations, asshole," he muttered.

Silver hurried from the store, drink in hand, and cut a glance back: the clerk was off the telephone and wiping the counter with a wad of napkins. Full of bluff, he hadn't called the police after all. But Silver fixed his attention on his reflection in the glass front and understood what the clerk meant: droplets of blue dye—his melted drink—clung to his beard. He wiped them from his beard as he started his quick-paced jaunt, dropping the straw into the gutter when he came upon another set of industrious red ants. "Let's share," Silver offered and laughed at how the little guys would turn blue from an overpriced sugary drink.

★

Silver did business at Magic Money, though the exchange did cost a pretty penny—10 percent of the face value of his first paycheck in god knows how many years. But Silver was not upset because his pockets bulged with a little more than two thousand dollars, an amount he assumed was reserved for thieves and merchants, such as the fellow at the 7-Eleven. Plus, he didn't remember doing the work, so to him it was like free money. And even if he had remembered the work, the "work" was just the vague poetic words with which he perfumed the classroom air.

Silver stationed himself on the sidewalk, indifferent to the sun dropping blood-red behind the sign at the gas station across the street. And he didn't marvel at the crows yakking in a nearby jacaranda tree, or the mother at the bus stop singing love words into the untainted ear of her baby. Let another iceberg break apart and the Amazon River boil with a chemical run-off and close up shop for good. Let bears go into hiding and the waterfowl waddle into dirty zoos. Silver

was dazed by money and for a brief moment could understand a Republican's complaint about taxes. Why hadn't he
seen that before? He himself was scandalized by all the
deductions from his salary—what was this one about FICA
and Medicare? The working man was being royally robbed!
A car's honk, however, brought him out of his daze.

"Chump Republicans!" he blared to the wind of traffic.

Silver kicked a stone. He was embarrassed by his brief lapse
from all he had lived for, namely a good time with plenty of
beer and, every fourth year when Republicans resurfaced in
office, his call to arms in the guise of political poetry. He
returned to himself, all 135 pounds, and decided to splurge
recklessly at the Denny's next to the gas station. He hitched
up his loose pants and crossed the street against a red light.

The Denny's was nearly vacant. His smile attracted the
waitress, a tired soul with ketchup on her apron, and some
on her bonnet, which was deflated from the sweaty sprints
from one sticky table to another.

"Just one?" she asked, sounding almost disappointed.

"Just one," Silver chirped, happy to seat himself in a booth.

Silver ordered a hot Super Bird turkey sandwich and a
strawberry shake thick as wet cement. It was over this lone
early dinner that Silver chose his path: he would continue
teaching. After all, the money was too good. Where else
would he get the perks of free pencils and pens, envelopes,
paper, paper clips of varying sizes, and an audience to listen
to his poetry? Jesus, I have it made, he reflected, and savored a
forkful of turkey meat. A hungry man, he ate without looking
up. When he was down to sucking the colored toothpicks that
came with his dinner, he patted his belly, presently an upheaval
of digestion, and weighed the risks: he was bedding down with

the college president's wife and had to regulate the moodiness of a troubled student in his class. Also, there was that teary-eyed woman with the batch of poems. But he assured himself that he could control them all and smarten up on basketball lingo for the fall season—boy, the cheerleaders were something! He sipped iced water and sucked on his strawberry shake, draining it like a swamp. He tasted the aftereffects of his meal when he smacked his lips and felt a sugar rush build up his confidence. What was his problem, really? Sip, sip from his water glass. He stroked his beard reflectively as he saw himself facing a problem most of his chums back in Oakland would envy. A job, that is. He had it made in the shade—just go to class, avoid Laura and the woman with the poems, and—oh, yes—please his landlady, Mrs. Bartlett, by eating her apple pie under the Mount Rushmore of Ronald Reagan's portrait.

For the road, he ordered two donuts, which he hooked on his thumb. He exited Denny's, patting his stomach, and walked in the direction of the college, all uphill. But Silver was too happy to complain. He munched on the donuts until they were gone and sucked his sugar-glazed thumb like a baby. Life was just too sweet!

As it was twenty to four, Silver returned to campus, where, at the bookstore, he bought a pullover shirt and socks, both on sale and sporting logos of the college. Silver would later nibble the logos like a convict until his teeth were full of thread. But for the time being, he had to rid his body of his Hawaiian shirt and socks as they were both embedded with powerful human smells. He also purchased breath mints, a packet of disposable razors, and a new wallet to hold his cash. He paid cash and left the store, whistling.

In the men's room, he splashed like a duck at the basin

and changed into his new clothes, which he modeled in the mirror over the sink. *Muy* ugly, he judged harshly. But he was pleased that the clothes gave off a newly purchased smell. He hailed into his mouth the pellets of white breath mints that would return him to the ranks of the human—the chow at Denny's had made him pipe up a series of burps. He lifted and appraised the disposable razors, weapons that could tear at his skin if he wasn't careful, as it had been several years since he brought one to his face. He intended to shave his beard, but would risk such a move at a later time—then again, he may keep his beard because he could always show off its electrical wattage if he were asked to read again. It was a tough choice, to shave and go naked-faced in public, or to hide, like a bandit, behind the shrubbery on his mug.

When he left the men's room and turned in to the commons area, he was confronted by Jason, his student, rocking back and forth on his skateboard. Startled, Silver nearly returned to the restroom to hide in one of the stalls. He dismissed this option, though. The young man's appearance prompted Silver to scoot away, silently he believed, but within seconds Jason was at his side, taunting him.

"Did you sell out, too?" the young man asked.

This accusation stopped Silver in his dusty tracks. Sell out! What did the little bugger know about "selling out"? As far as he could tell, he was the last true Chicano poet in *Aztlán*, though he had heard rumors that there were three or four in Texas, all of them sitting in public parks and, *carnales* to the end, sharing quarts of beer under shade trees. But he couldn't vouch for this piece of urban mythology.

"Who you callin' a 'sell-out'?" Silver's eyes, previously white, blazed red with anger.

The young man didn't back down. "I thought you were a true Hispanic?"

"Hispanic! Do I look like George W. Bush's kiss-ass, semibrown nephew?" His anger had roasted the breezy taste of his breath mints.

Jason twisted the chrome knob on his chin. He huffed and challenged Silver on another point. He barked, "How come you're wearing the sweatshirt?"

Silver peered down at the Simi Valley Baptist College logo of a smiling lamb. He had to admit that he appeared the lackey, a recently hired faculty member going with the flow. But not to be outdone by a kid on a skateboard, he spat out: "'cause, you little fool, it cost me only five dollars, and two for the socks." He wiggled the big toes of his feet. He next held up a paper bag that contained his Hawaiian shirt and socks. "You sniff these, and the funkiness will bend your nose for good, sucker!" His stomach acids were now hacking away at the recently devoured Denny's fare. "You don't know nothin' about me."

"I don't bathe either."

What? Was the kid agreeing with his funkiness? It had been a hot day, and he, a moving target, had been forced to run around under the magnifying glare of a southern California sun. Had he been emitting odors from head to foot?

Shoulders sagging, Jason shifted his interest. "My girl is mad at me because you didn't like my poem. She said that I should write better if I want her to like me."

Silver raised his head and regarded the merciless sky where, he suspected, no god dwelled on billowing clouds, but perhaps in a smoky comedy lounge. Maybe St. Peter was cracking a joke. Maybe St. Francis was laughing at the joke. No, to Silver the sky held clouds and smog and birds with

lice and ornithological ringworms. However, he saw that he
was dearly wrong. A plane was cutting across the yellowish
sky, and many feet above that plane a jumbo jet was crammed
with hostages pounding small plastic forks on their meal
trays and demanding more food and drink. The wind was
picking up, rattling the sharp-edged leaves of the eucalyptus.
The sun was nearly gone, but by the light that reflected off
the library he knew what to answer. He became philosophi-
cal. "Why don't you get a new girlfriend?"

Jason, head lowered, sniveled, "'cause they're all taken."

"They're all taken?" Silver pulled on his beard, lightly,
for he didn't deserve the punishment of a kid who had yet to
learn that nothing came easy in life. In fact, most of what
one wanted never arrived. "You're spoiled, Jason."

"Someone has to be, or what are Hispanics going to write
about?"

Silver couldn't stomach the lame response and walked
away, half-expecting the kid to follow on his skateboard. He
was relieved that he didn't sidle up next to him because he
would have smacked him one. Pissed, Silver couldn't believe
what he had heard: What are Hispanics going to write about?
¡Estupido!

Before heading home, he had to visit his office. He was
craving a couple of pens and a pad; he sensed the poetry of
anger rising like steam within him. He would gather the work
tools of a poet and sit in Mrs. Bartlett's backyard and write
until the only light he had to compose under was the cold,
cold stars. But as he fit the key into his office door, a voice
sounded: "Where is it, motherfucker?"

Silver recognized the voice. But how did the voice emerge
without a telephone? Did it come from a loudspeaker? The

comedy lounge in heaven? Yes, was St. Peter cracking a joke? Silver interpreted this unidentified voice as an anomaly; then, hand stroking his beard, he considered the possibility that his hearing had become acute since the typewriter fell on his head, and he had now been given the super power of hearing through doors, albeit ones with hollow centers. If so, he was going to put this talent to good use when he got back to Oakland. Silver chuckled. He realized his silliness. Professor Petersen probably had a speakerphone set up that kicked on after the fifth ring. He swung open the door of the office, expecting another round of "Where is it, motherfucker?" to come from the telephone on the desk.

But Silver was wrong. It was coming from right behind him. When he turned, he was confronted by a short man with a gun in his hand. The gun was black and stylishly color-coordinated with his black suit, shoes, and Alpine hat. Silver didn't need a push to step into the office; instead, he nearly ran, arms flapping like the wings of a fluttering chicken. He didn't cluck, though, when the man closed the door behind him and the last rays of sunlight vanished and the room darkened with heavy shadows.

Silver issued a nervous, "Hey, what's up with the gun?"

"Up your ass if I don't get it!" The man flicked on the overhead light and took a step toward Silver. "Sit down, professor!"

Silver obliged, his hands slowly lowering to rest in his lap. The man sniffed the air. "What smells?"

It was true after all. He had been throwing off a body odor that made people twitch their noses, rabbitlike, and perhaps privately gag when his back was turned.

"It's been a hard day," Silver answered after he smacked his lips for moisture. Fear had a way of drying his throat and lips, and they were dry now.

The man smiled widely, his coated tongue gray as a mouse. He repeated slowly, "A hard day? A hard day at the office?"

Silver was going to recount his trek to get his check cashed, but remained mum. He braced himself and cupped his hands into his armpits—perhaps that position might stop the flow of B.O. He spoke up. "What do you want?"

"You want to know what I want? What, are you a joker?" He took a seat and rested his gun on his lap, the barrel aimed at Silver's navel. "I want an A in the class." He chuckled and pushed his hat back so that his broad forehead showed. He pulled at a tear that parked itself in the corner of one eye, and soon reigned in his chuckle. "I want the kilo that was promised me."

Kilo?

"You and your fishing buddy were supposed to deliver last week."

Fishing buddy?

"Don't act dumb!" His face had darkened with wrath. "You and your amigo were supposed to fly his plane in on Friday and deliver my cut on Sunday before you went to church."

Silver turned, chair squeaking, and eyed the photograph of smiling Professor Petersen holding up his trout. Silver was learning something every day. While this was a Baptist college, there abounded weaknesses of the flesh, uncivil banter from the students, and malfeasance from its employees. The professor was dealing. Silver turned to the man with the gun, and swallowed. "Well, friend—what is your name again?"

"Let's not get chummy, asshole." Gun posted, finger on the trigger, he rolled his chair closer to Silver, braked with the heels of his shoes, and cried, holding his nose, "Jesus, it's you!" He used his feet to push away in his chair as far as he could go, which was the door with a poster of James Joyce, another stinker from another time.

Silver was aware that the man was not calling him Jesus. No, the man was accusing him of stench. He had to agree that the day had wrung from him his manly juices, in addition to plain fear. God, if he could only have learned from those little ants he had encountered earlier in the day. They were steadfast workers with no dreams except to lift Popsicle sticks and the like. Of course, their lives would be short and sweet if a human shoe landed on their heads.

"You got the wrong guy," Silver argued, then dirtied the air even more with a fib. "My name is George Moreno. I just took this gig for the spring."

The man narrowed an eye. "What are you talking about?"

"Petersen's on sabbatical." Silver didn't mean to snitch on the guy, but it was the truth.

Not a bright student of academic lingo, the man sat up. "Don't get smart with me, you worm. What's sabbatical?"

Silver explained that after three or four years of teaching, a professor got time off to write a book or travel for research. But, in a whisper, Silver confessed that most of them hung out the couch eating potato chips and watching afternoon TV. Or so he had heard.

The man huffed. He offered his opinion that if that was what a college professor did, the sabbatical thing, it was a racket if there was ever one. But he didn't give a shit. He wanted his kilo.

"But I'm not Petersen. I don't know what you're talking about."

The man removed his finger from the trigger. "Yeah, when I saw you, you didn't look like a Petersen. You looked Hispanic."

Silver bit his tongue as he fought the urge to lecture his assailant on the difference between Chicano and Hispanic, Hispanics being Republicans and Chicanos being Democrats, mainly. But he checked himself because the man had rolled his chair and taken Silver by the neck of his new sweatshirt. He wrenched the collar. "OK, Georgie boy, I want my kilo, and I don't give a rat's turd if you're not Petersen."

To Silver, the man didn't smell like an armful of roses, either. Some foul growth was lodged in his armpits.

"I can't help you."

"And why's that, Georgie boy?"

Silver nearly permitted his lips to flap the story of how the typewriter fell on his head and did away with both his short- and long-term memory. But his explanation would have come off as a lunatic's babble. Then he remembered: Hell, I don't know where Petersen lives. The guy might have boarded the plane with his friend and flown to Mexico for good. He said as much to the intruder.

"Then get his address, professor, or the next time it's going to be worse than this!" The man stood up, releasing his hold on Silver's sweatshirt.

Silver tried to iron out the wrinkles on the front of his sweatshirt. He was disturbed that his new clothes were already rumpled, and he had had them on no more than fifteen minutes. Slowly raising his eyes, he asked innocently, "Worse than what?"

The blackness of the gun butt introduced Silver to a deeper blackness as he rolled out of the chair and hit his head on the floor.

Chapter Seven

Silver lay on his back, mouth open to dust, bacteria, and the tepid morning sunlight that poured in from the parted blinds, when the door to his office opened with a squeak. Early-bird students could be heard in the courtyard; a mower was slaughtering the dew-moistened lawn. A trombone was bellowing in the distance, and a land-locked seagull answered its call.

"Oh," he managed to utter feebly. He raised his left arm, thin as the appendage of a praying mantis, and rested it in the valley of his stomach. He motored his other arm and rested that, too, on his stomach. He assumed the posture of a person in his coffin. But Silver was far from dead, though his pulse had slowed in pushing its cargo of blood through the peninsulas of his body. He struggled to raise his suffering head, his mouth shutting briefly like a Venus flytrap because he wasn't prepared for the intruder—Laura—to bring her mouth to his and continue where they'd left off a day ago with a huge suctioning kiss. When she let go of his lips after a nibble or two, he coughed from the overpowering scent of her perfume. He coughed a second time. Let her think that he had a cold and she might fear opening her throat to germs or, at least, the skunky bad breath of a middle-age man who had not yet had the chance to apply the morning toothbrush to his teeth.

"Close the door," Silver moaned.

"You read my mind, dirty boy!" Laura sang as she got up

from her knees and slammed the door, the draft of which sent dust in his direction. She stationed herself in front of him, hands on hips. She was wearing a sailorlike cap, a pleated sailor skirt, and a scarf around her neck. Her shoes were red pumps a size too small, thus killers if she had to trek more than a block or two. It appeared that she had done just that: her face was red and her breath was all but gone. Still, she remained fresh in appearance, cute even in her Popeye-the-Sailor outfit.

Silver could do no more than issue a second but louder "Oh." He had given up on the coughing tactic.

Laura responded to the call that she interpreted hastily as "Let's Get It On." She pushed away from the door, undid the anchor-looking buttons on her blouse, thus exposing the sail of a monstrous bra, and stepped out of her red pumps. Her tongue, a bud of pleasure, was wetting her lips for a big smooch.

"No," he protested weakly.

Laura posted her hands on her hips. "No? No to the captain of your bony little ship? Is this mutiny, ensign?" She chuckled, hands coming together for a light applause at her humor. Then her hands flew to her mouth. "Oh, my god!"

What god is she referring to, Silver wondered. The cad who wrote the Kama Sutra? While he was dizzy and wounded, he knew all about Laura, lusty wife of a small-framed Baptist college president with a pencil-thin tie. And while she was a large woman, she was enormously pliable, not unlike those women in the Kama Sutra, all bent and splayed, some with legs lifted effortlessly over their heads. Still, he was moved by her concern that he was supine and had a new head wound.

"You're bleeding, Silver." She went down to her knees

and, careful not to get her hands soiled with blood, used a pencil to push Silver's head to the side to inspect the wound. The wound was purplish but stamped closed with a soft scab. With the pencil, she stirred the nearly dried puddle of blood that stained the floor. "Shit, Silver, you're hurt!"

To Silver, her voice roared like a scold. Was she disappointed that he couldn't roll onto his belly, undo his Brown Power belt buckle, and perform his usual feat of Chicano horniness?

Laura hurled the pencil onto the desk. She slapped her hands of dust and adjusted her sailor's cap.

Silver sat up in a yoga position. "It's *nada*. I can still move my arms." He squeezed his hands into fists, breathed in and out so that the scaffolding of his chest rose and fell, and wiggled his toes. He observed with gratitude his body obeying what he regarded were telepathic commands. "I love you, toes! Oh, fingers, you point the way!" But, soon, concern overwhelmed him as he realized how close he had come to death. What if his assailant had targeted a truly mighty blow to his temple? Wouldn't he have succumbed and been no more than fodder for hungry ol' earth? And the shame of it! He, a corpse wheeled away from a Baptist college! What would his friends think, that is, the ones who could read and were partial to obituaries of literary figures? Nearly teary-eyed, he appreciated his body parts more than ever and praised, in particular, his lungs, concertinas that wheezed daily for his benefit. After all, didn't those spongy organs provide the means to suck in air, albeit polluted, into his body? He was going to treat his body parts to a hot bath later. For his head, he was going to search the drawers for a Band-Aid and aspirin.

Laura struggled to her feet. "Silver, I can't see you anymore if things keep falling on your head."

"I can't help it."

"No excuses." She glared at him for a long minute and then burst out crying. Her tears produced a flash flood that filled the gullies on each side of her nose. Her eyes became red; her mouth loosened into the pouty ugliness of a giant sea bass. In this state, she lost a little of her perfumy scent.

Silver was impressed by her display of emotions; he didn't know that she had it in her, the tears, the heartbreak, the sobbing that made her mascara run like sludge. He felt deeply for her, and, to his surprise, his heart ached. She was a large, sexy woman who had married too young. For twenty years she'd been part of a religion that frowned on beer and hard liquor and adultery in faculty offices. Then again, he thought, maybe her horoscope for the day read something like, "Dramatic scene with a poet goes nowhere. Move on." Still, he was moved by her tears.

"Don't cry," Silver cooed.

"Shut up!" Laura snapped.

He did.

During the silence between them, he lay back down, hands on his stomach. To improve his mood, he recalled the lunch at Denny's. Got to think of something, he told himself, and why not food? He pictured the hot turkey sandwich with steam rising like a genie, the goo of melted Swiss cheese cascading from the patty, the umbrellalike parsley, the limp pickle, and the finger-length French fries bloodied with ketchup. He was placing a strawberry shake into the picture when Laura scolded, "Quit sleeping!"

Silver sat up, a dead man in his coffin. He appeared

startled, but felt limp, as after a strong massage.

"You're not paying attention to me!"

Silver watched her cry a little more, though he suspected the last blast of tears were forced, unsalted, and lukewarm.

After she controlled herself and did away with her messy mascara with Kleenex, she announced, "We have to stop anyhow. I think Wesley knows."

"Oh, Christ," Silver moaned. He envisioned himself impaled on a spit turned by a jury of Baptist elders in poor-fitting suits. He wondered whether there was a loophole once a sinner was caught.

"He really doesn't know, but I want to tell him. He's a good person, but boring!" She drained the gullies a second time with a wipe of her thumb. She reached for her blouse on the chair. "You don't want to run away with me, do you?"

Run, yes, he confessed to himself. But with you? God, no.

"You're a coward!"

Silver ignored the proclamation. He slowly rose to his feet and carefully touched his forehead. He squinted his eyes closed as he recalled the blackness of the gun butt. He recalled the little man in the black suit and hat, and the insult that suggested that he—Silver—smelled of human stench. But Silver had a concern larger than his funkiness.

"Where does Professor Petersen live?"

Laura, buttoning her blouse, snapped, "You don't love me!"

"Laura, I'm in trouble."

"And I'm not? I'm in this marriage I don't want to be in!" Her anger steamed her cheeks and the remaining flecks of tears. Indeed, salt deposits formed small rings on her skin.

"A guy came here and smacked me in the head with a gun."

"And you don't think I hurt!" she screamed, stomping

first her left pump, then her right, a tango of anger that Silver couldn't duplicate in his worn huaraches. She remarked haughtily that he needed someone to knock some sense into him. Didn't he know that he was loving a very special woman! She pushed out her chest and her bosom rose like the Persian Empire. "You'll miss not getting to taste these anymore, buddy boy!"

"But it wasn't my fault." He cast a sad good-bye to her breasts. Yes, he was already regretting not being able to wet his whistle on those mounds. In particular, he was partial to her left breast, but either one did the trick.

"Every time I want to make love, you have to ruin the mood by getting hurt and bleeding. What's wrong with you? Don't you know how to love a woman?"

Love a woman? Of course he did! He had to admit, however, that he was out of practice, and his back hurt from assuming the man-on-the-bottom position. But he took pride in pleasing a woman. After all, didn't he sport a Brown Power belt buckle? Didn't that say it all?

"Laura, listen to me," he pleaded. "Please don't tell Wesley."

Laura promised nothing. She was out the door, the engine of her immense bottom picking up speed as she hurried across the courtyard, shoving her bulk through a knot of students who were rehearsing a play. Silver was surprised that the weight of her anger didn't kick up sparks from her tiny pumps. He closed the door behind her and squinted at the poster of James Joyce. He had to wonder why the old master sported an eye patch. Did an Irish wench smack him a good one, or, in his time, did a little man in a black suit and black hat knock him with a gun butt? He sensed he was standing before an oracle. Mr. Joyce? he dearly wanted to ask on his knees. What's the answer to a woman who blames you for things that fall on your head?

Head bowed, his thumb and index finger tweaking his beard into place, he circled the room for an answer. But he halted abruptly.

"¡*Chingao!*" Silver roared. He began to pat his front and back pockets, frantically as if his pants were on fire. The wad of money from his first paycheck in years was gone. He turned his pockets inside out: they hung like tongues on his thighs. He stuffed the tongues back into his pants and let out a whimper, then a naughty word, and then a whimper that had him sitting in Professor Petersen's chair.

"It's your fault, dude!" he yelled at the photo on the desk. He picked up the photo, his fingerprints greasing the glass, and would have crashed it against the wall but feared the flying glass would strike back in vengeance, piercing his skin like arrows. He was already having a bad-luck day. Instead, he sobbed, "I've been robbed!"

As an Oakland resident, Silver had been robbed in the past by thugs who leapt from behind trees like shadows. But what did they get? Usually a couple of dollars, a roll of breath mints, cigarette lighters, BART tickets, crushed joints, and groceries that amounted to domestic beer and tiny bags of barbecue potato chips, his favorite empty-calorie snack. But two thousand dollars? Never. In Simi Valley, crime was serious.

Silver reached for the telephone and dialed the one campus number that might be of immediate service: the number was on the manuscript of poems submitted to him for appraisal by that woman—what's her name?—he had encountered after his reading. The one who prodded him into the hallway and down the hallway. The one whose parents had been missionaries?

"The president's office," the voice answered.

Silver stuttered, he clucked, he wheezed. Finally, he let out a shallow "aah," the last word of a drunk falling from a ten-story building in a seedy part of a town decent citizens avoided.

"Professor Mendez, is that you?" the voice asked none-too-nicely.

His memory could not provide her name. Then he quickly turned to the folder that held her poems. Ah, yes. "Mildred, I'm really sorry about yesterday afternoon. I promise to look at your poems. Right now I need Professor Petersen's home number."

"Why?"

Why?

He swiped a paper clip from the desk, plied it open nervously, and commenced to bend it back and forth in a sort of calisthenics work out. With such action, his fingers might put on an ounce of flesh, a prerequisite to writing a novel or filling out a long application form for a job at Penney's. "'Cause he and I are . . . working on a conference."

"He never told me about anything like that."

Silver's nose grew as he concocted a long—and lame—fib. "'Cause it's a secret. We don't want our students to know."

"Then who's going to this conference if not students? Pigeons?"

Silver swallowed, his body awash with sweat from the interrogation. "The people."

Cruel laughter.

"The people? People don't read. They like to eat Cheetos and get fat!"

Silver withered. Exhausted, temples thumping, he let go of the barbell-shaped paper clip. Fuck the novel! Fuck the job application form! Still, he continued because his money was gone and he needed it back. Otherwise he might have to remain in Simi Valley. "Yes, and that's why . . . we're having the conference."

Mildred responded with a growl. She suggested that he open the drawer of his desk, where he would locate his address and telephone number on any one of his college business cards. She next informed him that President Skaggs wanted to see him.

"Why?"

"Maybe it's about the conference!" With that, she slammed the phone down, but not before crying that she had stopped writing poetry for good and it was all his fault.

"Jesus," Silver groaned, Roto-Rootering a finger in the ear that suffered her tirade. Before he abandoned his position at the college, he was going to recommend to the administration anger-management classes for staff.

When the telephone rang again, Silver imagined it was the man in the black suit, the asshole with his money. He imagined socking him a good one in his kisser. When he picked it up, Mildred's voice sounded: "I forgot to tell you. I have your check."

Silver sat up, confused. "Didn't I just get paid?"

"Yes, but that was a check for your *first* month, and this one is for your *second* month."

Silver recalled something about not getting paid right away—the college was so sorry about the screw-up, etc.— and this second check must have just been cut.

"Can you hold it for me, Millie?" Silver didn't want this

check snatched from him.

"'Mildred,' Professor Mendez," she corrected coolly. "My writing name is Mildred and my public name is Mildred. Millie is a name reserved for mules!"

Touchy!

Instead of continuing the debate over Mildred versus Millie, Silver promised to take the poems to bed and read them in the solitude of evening. After all, she did have his check, and she might hold it in front of him like a carrot— he the mule with bared teeth snapping for his veggie.

"You're taking my poems to bed?" Mildred asked haughtily. "How dare you!"

Silver gulped what spittle remained in his mouth. "It's a figure of speech, Millie."

"You have a dirty mind!" she shouted and hung up.

Silver touched the side of his head, which bonged with a headache. But he didn't have time to complain. He found a box of his business cards, pulled two out—one went immediately into his pants pocket—and dialed the number. He got an answering machine, which prompted an outburst from Silver: "Shit, don't people answer their fuckin' phones no more!" He left a message for Professor Petersen to give him a call.

As he hung up, a knock sounded at the door.

Silver grew church-mouse quiet because he didn't wish to see a visitor at that moment, when he was broke and broken. He probed the wound near his temple; dried blood like bark. He peeled the slop of a fitful sleep from the corners of his eyes. He frowned at the blood splattered on his new sweatshirt. He had to admit to shabbiness. What could he do but forge his fingers into a comb and rake his hair and beard? About his breath, he could do nothing. But he was tempted to nibble on a pencil, and if he had to part with a response longer than a "Yes" or "No," he might get away with his breath smelling like wood shavings.

The knock pecked again.

His breathing slowed, but the squeak of the chair gave him away. When the knock sounded again, he called, "Yes?"

"It's me," a young-person's voice called.

Other than that it was young and meek, not the boisterous bellow of either Laura or Mildred, the female voice was unfamiliar. He pulled his beard for an answer as he rummaged his memory for a soft-spoken woman. But it became clear all too quickly. In bounced Amber, his cheerleading student, and, in fact, clad in her cheerleading attire made of skimpy polyester. A pair of pom-poms were pressed to her bosom. Her ponytail was a whip that might bring down the holiest of men.

"Good morning!" Amber chimed.

Silver was sorely aware of the time of day, though he had yet to stretch like a cat or rinse his mouth or wash his face or even peel the blood from the side of his head. He put himself on alert that he probably smelled funky. He also warned himself not to speak too loudly; he would scare her away with his breath. He had to make at least a couple of friends on this campus, and couldn't it be with students such as Amber?

"Professor!" One of Amber's pom-poms went sweeping to her face as if they were playing peek-a-boo.

I haven't spoken a single word, Silver rued, and she's already critiquing my halitosis. And what would she think if she took a microstep toward him and evaluated his B.O.? He kept his arms at his side. He would hate to open them like wings and really end their relationship. Through nearly closed lips, he mumbled, "What?"

"You've got blood on your head." The pom-pom dropped. Her face held the worry lines of a bad actress. Then the worry lines disappeared, and her freshness returned as she cut a glance to the door and prophesied, "I'll come back later. When you're not . . . bleeding." She brought from beneath the shaggy head of her pom-pom what Silver imagined to be a love letter; it was folded many times, a carry-over from elementary school when notes were passed from hand to hand? She told him it was a poem for class and tossed it like a paper airplane onto the desk. She was out the door, her tiny dress swirling and a few streamers from the pom-poms floating to the floor.

Silver got up and closed the door behind her, but not before peeking out and observing the thespians rehearsing a play. But when he realized that they weren't reading a play but the Bible aloud to each other, he shut the door.

"God help me," Silver whispered. He turned, picked up and unfolded the poem on the desk, and gazed at the girlish handwriting on lined paper. The title read "Memories."

"Oh, yeah," he reminded himself. He recalled the night before at the basketball game, how she had informed him while jigging from one tender foot to the other that she was working on a poem or had finished a poem or was a poem herself, all grace and fine lines. While the marching band played, she threw one leg into the air, then the other, thus exposing not so much her panties but Silver's resolve to not explore the tempting display. Silver would have dwelled dreamily on the soft-porn memory but the telephone rang. He stared at it. It's Mildred, he guessed. No, the guy in the black suit. No, Laura. No, Wesley with Laura. Silver swallowed nervously. He assumed that she had spilled the beans to Wesley, the whole enchilada, like times and places and who came first. Perhaps even the business of wiping away their butt and handprints with the little rake from the hall closet.

"Yeah," he said, answering it.

"Silver Mendez?" the voice asked.

Professor Petersen.

"Yeah, it's me, and it's you, Petersen?" Silver asked.

"You called?"

Silver stood up, legs splayed as he was determined to get tough. "Yeah, I called. First your fuckin' typewriter falls on my head and then your little friend comes over and whacks me for good measure." Silver splayed his legs wider. He was through with being played with. "You dealing, Homes?"

"What are you talking about?"

"I'm talking about moving *mota* and maybe even toot. I'm talking about bleeding in two places, and neither is my mouth or my asshole, asshole!"

Petersen remained quiet. There was no force behind his words when he said, "You don't have to use that tone of voice on me. After all, I helped you get the job."

Get the job?

"Listen, man, I've been here two months and what do I have to show for it? Knots on my head and my money is gone. Plus—" Silver hesitated. He was smart enough not to bring up Laura or, for that matter, Mildred. "I know what you're up to, and I ain't talkin' about your middle-class, crybaby poems. You're dealing shit on the side."

Petersen protested and assured him that he voted Republican in the last four elections. He argued that he was all for President Bush's strategy on the war on terrorism. A long pause followed. Then he whispered, "Silver, you want some? I can get you some toot for free."

Silver snapped a pencil in two. "Nah, man, my intake is through my mouth. Nothing goes up my nose except smells. And right now, Homes, you smell."

Silver scolded Petersen for five minutes until Petersen began to cry.

They made a date for high noon at the Denny's on Marshall Street. Petersen asked if Silver knew the place.

"You bet I do," Silver retorted angrily. He touched his empty stomach, a valley even standing up. "But let's make it two. I got to teach your class." He had the class, but also Mildred's poems to read. If he didn't read them, he would never get his check.

He hung up and stared at the folder that contained Mildred's poem. He just woke up and didn't want to go back to sleep reading poetry written by a spinster who drank vinegar morning, noon, and night. Then he heard his stomach rumble on its slather of emptiness. He looked up at the clock: 10:37.

"Ah, just get it over with," he told himself and threw open the folder. The first poem was titled "Memories."

Chapter Eight

As Silver sized up his tuna sandwich, dented with fingerprints from when the cook sliced it in half, his stomach rumbled, his tongue rose and fell like a whale, and his mouth gushed with saliva. But these bodily responses to his first meal of the day had to wait. Alert as a fox, Silver raised his eyes when he heard plodding footsteps and summarily sized up a man who could only be Petersen. He was dressed in a fishing jacket—a couple of bright lures were attached to his vest like war medals. His hat jingled with lures, too, plus a Bush/ Cheney campaign button. Something's fishy, Silver told himself, and it wasn't the tuna sandwich. No, it was the guy extending a hand, the guy with a smile.

"Silver," Petersen greeted heartily. "Good to see you."

Good to see you?

Silver thought: I need control. I need control and my money back. He slipped a pickle into his mouth and let it lie on his tongue like a host. The moment was anything but religious. He strangled his paper napkin and kept his temper boiling under his scalp.

"Sit down, man," Silver said sharply.

Silver had it all planned. He had concocted in his mind a story he was sure would make Petersen open his billfold and eagerly pull out all his greenbacks. It was a story about drug runners found floating in dirty canals outside Los Banos with bullet wounds in the back of their heads and one behind the ear for good measure. Petersen would shit his pants—or at least fart heartily the winds of fear—and eagerly hand over whatever money he had in his wallet and maybe some of what was sitting on his chest of drawers.

Petersen slid into the booth.

Silver chomped on a serrated pickle and the sourness made him think of Mildred. He didn't have time to see Mildred about his other paycheck, but once it was pocketed, he was going to slap his butt in a sort of giddyap and ride out of Blanche. Let the college search for him in Oakland if it thought he hadn't completed his tour of duty. He had served his two months as professor and had the knots on his head to prove it. He had had enough, though he would always retain a soft spot for Amber's legs.

"So how's teaching?" Petersen asked.

Silver ignored Petersen's chummy attitude. When his stomach rumbled for attention, he set his eyes on his sandwich, the cleanest thing in Denny's. He had noticed the carpet was smeared with dropped French fries, the booths were sticky, and on the windowsill a single lunatic fly was on its back, occasionally buzzing its greasy wings. As for the *Mejicano* with a dirty mop, the dude was just swabbing bacteria from one part of the floor to the other.

"I ordered myself something," Silver informed Petersen. "The tuna salad's out of a can, but what isn't these days?"

Petersen nodded. The nod attracted a waitress with an apron splattered with ketchup, mustard, and grease stains. It had been a long shift for her. Shadows were deep under her eyes. Her stockings were clawed with runs from bumping into chairs, tables, and belligerent toddlers. She didn't bring out a pad when Petersen ordered a Coke and a straw.

"Thank you," the waitress said. She was happy the order

could be gripped in one hand. Still, she bartered, "Got apple and rhubarb pie if you want."

Petersen worked up a false smile. His answer was in his fangs.

Silver considered the guy oily, unlike the tuna sandwich that he brought to his face. Silver chewed with his mouth closed. He thought: control, just get back your control. To get to that position where he was calling the shots, he sipped his iced tea and became abrupt. "You're dealing, and you're in trouble, man."

Petersen's smile collapsed at the edges. Still, his eyes showed confidence as the smile lifted. His fangs showed themselves when he protested, "You got it all wrong, Silver. I'm not what you think."

Silver sighed and pointed at the tuna sandwich. "You want to be like this guy? Dead on a plate?"

"I pay my taxes."

Pay my taxes?

"What does that have to do with anything?"

"I'm American."

American?

It occurred to Silver that this goofball was unreachable. He turned his face away, as if he had just been slapped, and labored to find meaning beyond the plate-glass window of Denny's. In the reflection, he could see Petersen sag; he was less confident, less alive than five minutes ago. The man was scared, and it showed in the pleats on his forehead. Silver wondered if once you were dead the pleats ironed out with time.

Petersen gulped and changed the subject. "Habla español?"

"Fuck *habla español*!" Silver had been in such a good mood. After all, he had before him a tuna sandwich with potato chips piled at the side like debris. Now a novice drug runner sat before him, both hands on his small potbelly, evidence that the man ate three square meals a day. He leaned toward Petersen, who was suddenly jittery, as if in his blood surged the cocaine he was peddling on the side. In a whisper, Silver predicted the future: "You're dead when you don't deliver."

Rumors abounded from the living; the dead didn't have much to report. Silver had heard that drug runners in Oakland would take toenail clippers to your private parts and butcher them all the way down to the hairs—no worry about testicular cancer after that kind of shaving. Others would set you on fire. Still others lowered a weed eater to your back and watched gleefully as the skin came off in nice strips. The sane ones just put a bullet in you, then went and had a lunch of gumbo and crackers. When Silver told as much to Petersen, his fanged smile collapsed for good.

"Do you really think they'll hurt me?" Petersen asked, lower lip trembling. Letting his head sink, his eyes disappeared beneath the brim of his hat. "It wasn't my idea."

Silver bit into his sandwich. His jaws worked pensively on the bread and tuna, and his tongue scooted the cheese from his back molars. He sipped his iced tea. Life was good in spite of his guest, a weak link in the drug trade. "It wasn't your idea? What, did some Hispanic bring you into moving drugs?"

Petersen's eyes reappeared and a grin made a new hole on his face. His confidence rose like a flower. "As a matter of fact that's how it happened."

Silver set his sandwich down and dusted his hands free of breadcrumbs. Furious, he berated Petersen for blaming Hispanics for everything from the downturn of the economy to the energy crisis to pollution to streets throughout the state being renamed Cesar Chavez Boulevard. The businessmen who couldn't even say Chavez's name right had to spend money to replace their old stationery. Silver glared at Petersen's hat with the Bush/Cheney button.

"You look like a *pendejo*," Silver scolded. "Take that off! You're supposed to be a poet, not a billboard for those chumps"

Petersen, pride hurting, hesitated. But as Silver's anger intensified, he carefully removed his hat from his head; the fishing lures could bite from their own hunger. He shook his head and said, "I got talked into it."

"OK, what exactly is this thing called 'it'"?

Petersen touched the water ring of Silver's iced tea.

Silver slapped his hand like a child. "Quit fuckin' playing around! What did you do, man?"

Petersen stalled when the waitress approached with his drink.

"Anything else?" she asked. Her fingernails were bleeding ketchup.

The two shook their heads.

After the waitress set the bill down and left, he confided in whispers, "I met this guy named José but his real name might be Luís. He was from Lamont but lived in Burbank for a while. Said he was in the Mexican army, but I think he was lying—he had three fingers missing, and what kind of army recruits cripples?" His whisper then became almost a murmur. "Between you and me, the guy goes by Luís."

Oh brother.

Petersen, in a voice as flat as his poems, briefed Silver about how he and his buddy would often go fishing in northern California, on the Sacramento River. Trout mainly, but salmon in October at the Oregon border. His buddy piloted his own plane. During one of these trips, his buddy recounted a story of yet another buddy who would fly in cocaine for a fellow that everyone called Little Man. Petersen said that he and his buddy were flying quietly over Fresno when they shook hands on an illegal franchise between them.

"Is your buddy's sky ride a single or twin engine?"

Petersen tore at his napkin, nervously. "Single."

"Good," Silver answered. "If it had been a two-jobber, shit, man, he'd be running a huge load. Right now you got some José or Luís, whatever, and the dude's missing three fingers. Then you got your buddy and this little guy phoning every hour." Silver waited. He waited for Petersen to snitch on those enjoying the drugs.

When Petersen didn't speak up, Silver pried. "Come on, man, who gets the goodies to put up his nose?" He raised a potato chip. If Petersen answered the question, Silver would feed him a salty reward. After the silence between them grew, Silver tossed the potato chip into his own mouth, chomped, and swallowed. He restated his question, more or less. "Who are you selling to?"

Petersen shrugged like a little boy.

"Come on, you're speaking to a fellow poet."

"Everybody," Petersen answered finally.

Everybody?

Petersen repeated himself and described the bigger picture: "You know, it's recreational, people just having a good time." He boosted a smile on his face, but behind the smile there was no humor. He and his buddy, he said, were portrayed as hip in the eyes of their neighbors, hip because their hair covered most of their ears. His friend also had two studs in his right ear. Radical.

"You're hip?" Silver asked incredulously. "With that fuckin' hat of yours?" He took a sip of iced tea, crunched a sliver of ice, and inquired about his clients. "Are they like doctors and shit?"

Petersen nodded his head.

Silver fed himself a potato chip. "Optometrists, dentists, accountants with two sets of books—the cream of Blanche!"

Petersen shushed him. "You're not being fair."

Silver stabbed a finger into his own chest. Had it been a knife, blood would have spilled onto the carpeted floor—more work for the *Mejicano* with a mop. "I'm not being fair? Get real, man!"

"Hispanics can't have all the fun. These guys need drugs, too."

Silver beaded his eyes and brooded: This guy teaches? Silver clucked his tongue, through with Petersen. In his mind, he saw his body floating in a river with schools of revengeful fish nibbling at his toes. "You got a stupid problem I don't really want to know about. Right in your office I get mugged by some short shit in a black suit. Who's my witness but your posters of James Joyce and Whitman?"

Petersen laced his fingers into a steeple while his voice, earlier cracking with regret, turned to a malingering tenderness. "Silver, I know I should have alerted you. I was remiss. That wasn't decent of me." He explained that his buddy never returned from the last trip. The good citizens of Blanche, he claimed, were calling him—the engineers, the orthodontists, the lawyers, the plastic surgeons with their drawers full of drawings for new faces—all eager for little snort on the weekend, though some preferred the sweet scent of Humboldt County's best marijuana. Raw-nosed, they were, moreover, calling because some had invested thousands of dollars, and not for themselves but others. Some were scared that the police might step in and snoop.

Silver had heard that most cocaine-sniffing druggies weren't the dreadlocked brothers and young Latinos in hair nets, but professionals with damp underarms, the worst being accountants who had to crunch numbers all day. Now he could confirm the rumors. He took a drink of his iced tea. Discovering it unsweetened, he tossed two sugar cubes into the dark brew like depth charges. This was his own drug, sugar that in a few minutes would make his heart race and compel his knees to jump up and down under the table. For now, the sugar sweetened his breath and dispelled the fishiness of the tuna sandwich.

Petersen's steeple of righteous fingers collapsed when Silver informed his new friend that he was going to wake up dead.

"But I got a family."

"You'll still have a family, but they won't have you around."

Petersen tried to reconstruct the steeple, but it collapsed from worry.

"I should've known better than to stay around here. It's too dangerous. I'm going back to Oakland." He sucked on his iced tea. His breath cooled, but his anger remained for the lost paycheck, his first check in months. He had every intention of asking Petersen for the two thousand dollars, plus a ride to Burbank where he could catch a Greyhound bus. But he changed his mind; the guy had his own problems and Silver wouldn't want to be in the car when the supplier caught up with Petersen. The way things were going that scenario might occur sooner than later—followed by the *whack-whack* of an automatic at close range. Silver ate the rest of his sandwich, wiped his mouth and said, "You pay for this."

"Me?" Petersen's hands went to his chest, St. Sebastian with a little hurt.

"Shut up, man! And leave a good tip, too."

The waitress, he noticed, was stopping every now and then to adjust the stockings that had begun to puddle around her thick ankles. He felt pity. He imagined that such work was her punishment for marrying a poor man right out of high school. This is what Silver, poet of conjecture, supposed. He also supposed that he might get a few dollars out of Petersen, who had drawn his wallet from his back pocket.

"Gimme that!" Silver snarled. He ripped the wallet out Petersen's hands.

Petersen looked around, jaw slack. He protested, "You can't do that!"

Silver ignored his plea and plucked two dirty-faced twenties that had the stench of a smoky bar. He set the wallet on the table and slid it back to Petersen. He stood up and said, "You better take over my class because I'm leaving."

"But I'm on sabbatical!"

"Nah, man, you're on drugs."

★

Silver turned in the direction of his rented abode, Mrs. Bartlett's house, where he anticipated dreamily a utopia of robins, jays, and the lesser birds of the air gargling the leftover moisture of sprinklers that misted the lawns. But first he had to deal with being lost—the residential streets all looked the same. When a police cruiser crept by, he uttered an uncivil rant of "Oh, shit, *la chota*," and exercised great attention on a crack in the sidewalk. The crack resembled a line on his right palm that had yet to bring him fortune, though during his youth it often cupped the spillage of late afternoon ejaculations. He then bent down, fingers panto-miming the awkward action of a kindergartner tying shoelaces. But wearing loose huaraches, he had nothing to tie, nothing but a knot of fear in his stomach.

Finally, he found his bearings—the cross on President Skaggs's house a block away provided him direction—and soon located Mrs. Bartlett's house. And how could he miss it? There was the iron statue of the red-lipped Negro boy holding up a boot. But he hesitated as he reclaimed his conscience and remembered the dog he had secretly proclaimed his own. He hurried to the privet hedge where he expected to find the pooch. Indeed, the dog was still on his private bivouac, muck in his eyes and leaves caught in his floppy ears. Silver coaxed him from the hedge and prodded him along with the snap of his fingers. The dog trailed stiffly, head lowered and examining the march of his legs, apparently amazed that he could get about.

"You been to Oakland?" Silver asked.

The dog's tail wagged once.

"Oakland is like . . ." Silver fabricated the vision of comfy homes, he the salesman selling swamp land to an innocent party. He lurched forward with a tall tale as he described the city with its gentle rise and fall of green hills, which was true in places, and how its citizens, all liberals, drove Volvos. Oh, how privileged were the Irish Setters riding shotgun in those Volvos, the breeze of air conditioning animating their long fur. But the places that Silver frequented on tiptoe—East Oakland came to mind—were nothing like the rhap-sody of good, clean living. Plus, he had seen enough dogs lapping runoff in gutters or killed on roadsides, their paws thrust straight up into the air, their eyes dilated on a sky ribbed with clouds. He abandoned that grim landscape. No, he would feed the dog and feed himself with whatever foodstuffs he could grub from Mrs. Bartlett's refrigerator. The next morning, they would board a Greyhound bus, the limousine for the state's poor.

Silver prodded the dog through the side gate of Mrs. Bartlett's house, shushed him though he had yet to utter a single yap, and went inside none too comfortably. He closed the door behind him, calling timidly, "Hello? Mrs. Bartlett, it's only me." He intended to shower, cater tidbits for the dog from the refrigerator, rest one night, and then sneak out of town with the dog in tow. He would, however, return to campus to claim his paycheck from Mildred. Yes, he couldn't forget the paycheck!

Mrs. Bartlett was on the couch, a large-print *Reader's Digest* resting on her lap. By all appearances she was reading by the light of the Ronald Reagan portrait on the wall behind her—apparently she had moved it from the kitchen to where she sat. Reagan, the great communicator, was wearing a cowboy hat; his teeth, shiny and false, lit up the room.

"There you are," Mrs. Bartlett greeted. Her own teeth were false, but she wore no cowboy hat. "You didn't come home last night."

Silver bit his lower lip, punishment for the fib that he was about to construct. "Yeah, well, I was working on a poem that was longer than a snake."

Longer than a snake? What an awful metaphor!

He swallowed, admonishing himself for the use of an ugly metaphor, then continued, "I slept in my office. It was nice and cozy." True, he did sleep on the floor, but that catnap was induced by the violent end of a gun butt.

To Silver's stupefaction, Mrs. Bartlett's mouth appeared to masticate, but on what nutrition? Peanuts? A slice of apple. Or was it antacids? Bile that heaved itself when he first stepped into the room and she smelled him?

"Are you OK?" Silver inquired. He prayed that he would not have to do mouth-to-mouth.

She leveraged a frown for what Silver judged to be his clumsy lie about composing a poem as long as a snake. Then he realized that she was working her false teeth into place— the plate had fallen away from her gums. Her hand went up to her jaw for better control.

"Mrs. Bartlett, I was wondering . . ." His voice trailed off when he witnessed her grow in size and spring from the coach, albeit tottering as she shimmied for balance on the shaggy carpet. The force of her leap came not from her legs and arms but the couch, from a lever that thrust the bottom cushion upward. The cushion slowly receded hydraulically, with a light hum.

"Whee," Mrs. Bartlett cried, face lit with genuine happiness.

"Cool," Silver sang. He was awed by the device and would have given anything to have had a couch like that when he was a kid. The fun of being light enough to hit the switch and fly across the living room! Or, for that matter, he could use one as an adult—his drunk friends would welcome such help getting to their feet and tottering to the refrigerator for another round of cold ones.

Mrs. Bartlett tottered toward the kitchen and Silver followed her. She had apple pie and asked if he would like a piece, with milk, of course, or coffee, if he preferred. She turned and, hands clasped, said, "Oh, gosh, I need to go to the library."

Silver didn't know what to say.

"Can you drive me?"

Silver hadn't driven a car in years. And the last car he owned—a Buick with droopy headlights and a headliner like a fallen tent—he mostly pushed, a great American gas saver. God, how his legs and arms had become bulky with muscle! God, how he elicited crank gestures, the middle finger being the most common followed by "Get that piece of shit off the road, asshole!" Plus, there had been more than one riffraff brother who wanted to buy the parts—tires, radio, fan belt— as he pushed it along the street. Silver, however, preferred not to ponder those hurtful memories. He answered Mrs. Bartlett, "Yeah, I can drive." He almost added, "Push too," but withheld this piece of personal history.

Mrs. Bartlett spied the kitchen clock, an owl with swinging eyes. "It's after four. We better hurry. But we shan't be long."

While Mrs. Bartlett scooted off to her bedroom, Silver scavenged the refrigerator, the bulb like a flashlight in his face. And, in fact, his whole head was nearly in the refrigerator as he, a pirate, ransacked the meat drawer. Lucky him! There was prepackaged cooked sausage and baloney! He tore off a chunk of sausage and counted out eight slices of baloney. He hurried out the back door and to the side of the house. The pooch, head bent awkwardly, was licking the end of a leaky faucet.

"Little brother," he called to the dog. "*Comida* time!"

Kneeling, Silver held out first the sausage, which the dog nibbled politely, and then roughly when he caught on that a good meal was about to be had. He next dealt out the second course—four slices of baloney for the dog and four for Silver, he on his knees and the dog on his gimpy legs. Thus they ate on a Thursday when the sun was pulling its light westward above leaves guillotined by autumn and the shift of time.

Chapter Nine

Silver assumed that he would be driving to a small public library, but after Mrs. Bartlett instructed him to get her beast of an old Lincoln on the freeway he learned that they were going somewhere else. After the freeway and two dusty miles on a winding road into dry mountains, Silver pulled into a parking lot decorated with American flags and patriotic music booming from speakers hidden in trees. The place resembled a theme park. But where were those rides that dropped you a hundred feet and let you off wobbly-legged and wanting to barf cotton candy and Cracker Jacks? He gazed up into the rearview mirror. His landlady's face was pressed to the window.

"I didn't think it would be this busy," Mrs. Bartlett remarked.

The lines of tour buses puffed black diesel smoke. Beyond them were parked cars, most of them hung with handicapped placards. He took his own placard from the passenger seat and yoked it around the rearview mirror.

"Lord, help me," Silver muttered as he pulled into a parking space. He revved up the huge V-eight engine once and stopped it, thus cutting off at least half of southern California's greenhouse emissions.

Silver's jaw hung open. It closed, tightened, and petrified into rock when he found himself placing one foot, then the other, onto the pavement of the Ronald Reagan Presidential Library and Museum. He would rather have stepped in quicksand—Jesus, if his buds back in Hayward could see him!

"I thought we were going to the library?"

"This is the library," Mrs. Bartlett chirped. "I have to pick up something."

Silver, a chauffeur with an expired license, kept his grumbling to himself and closed the door after Mrs. Bartlett. He walked next to her, scared of the crowd. He was acquainted with the fact that Republicans ruled the politics of the day but didn't realize they existed in such numbers. He had certainly seen them on television, but for the most part they were foreign to him, like French people or baguettes. The buds that he hung with on park benches were Democrats, though few of them ever stopped drinking long enough to actually vote. Still, Silver couldn't say that he had ever really been among Republicans. Now surrounded by them, Silver marched in his smelly sweatshirt, dirty pants, and huaraches, marched toward a gate where congregated old, gut-heavy men dressed in shorts and white socks pulled to their knees. The women, also with their own guts, wore white slacks, pink tops, and scarves with the American flag. But they appeared as shapes and figures of what they were—hordes of bow-legged tourists from Colorado, Idaho, Florida, Indiana, and Texas.

"I'll just wait in the car?" Silver suggested as a way of an escape.

"No, I need your help." Mrs. Bartlett pouted.

Silver had no choice but to shrug the pistons of his shoulders and agree to help. But help do what?

At the entrance, he nearly broke his promise when he saw that the donation fee was five dollars. He wasn't about to pay a dime, let alone five bucks, for a Republican shindig. When he noticed a guard opening the exit gate for Mrs. Bartlett, an apparent VIP, Silver followed sneakily, convinced that the heavy hand of the law was going to clamp down on his shoulder. But he felt only a light sheen of sweat rise through his pores. His mouth became dry, his teeth a pair of tartar-plated castanets. But Silver admonished himself: don't be scared of these chumps! They can't go where I've been! He envisioned the Rescue Mission in Richmond at five o'clock when soup was ladled into plastic bowls and bread set on the table like stones. These Republicans never experienced the stench of men and women hovering over their meager feast, as the smacking of their toothless gums amplified their slurping. They don't know! Silver argued, they don't know!

He navigated his way through the crowd to the courtyard, where the racket of camera shutters filled the air. What they were photographing Silver wasn't able to fathom; his attention was drawn to the flags that were snapping like whips in the breeze. How did they do that? There didn't seem to be a wind. Silver, stopping in his tracks, placed a hand over his eyes, as a poetic vision descended on him. His world became dark in that halted state. He imagined immigrants hired to wave cardboard in the direction of the flags, the energy of their *frijoles* and tortillas propelling the movement of the flags. He placed himself among them, but held a canister of lighter fluid that he squirted at the flags. In his pants pocket lay a Zippo lighter. But before he could flick it, his vision disappeared as a tap on his shoulder requested his attention.

"Enjoy yourself, Professor," Mrs. Bartlett said. She told him that she had business to do as she walked toward a well-dressed man approaching her. The man smiled widely at Mrs. Bartlett and Mrs. Bartlett returned the greeting— one Republican meeting another.

Abandoned among Republicans, Silver grew scared. He

drifted toward the camera-clicking crowd. He observed that more than one patriot had tears pouring from their eyes as they stood in front of the eight-foot bronze statue of Reagan in a Western getup. Reagan was holding a hat; he was also going to hold up a fake smile until the end of time, Silver judged. One young woman, probably only two years old when Reagan was first elected president, was bawling her head off. Tears dropped like dimes from her freckled face.

"Oh, Jesus," Silver remarked loudly. "She gets off on this *hombre!*" Silver was often moved by the sight of gutter pigeons with splayed beaks and diseased eyes and how they marshaled their hope by warbling for human favors. Oh, how he remembered one miraculous pigeon in whose beak glowed a crushed but smoldering cigarette butt. To add to the unusual moment, the feathered creature was perched on a crushed beer can. Now there was a champ! A bird for him.

Silver made his way into the library, a chill riding his arms from the air conditioning. In the foyer, he wandered aimlessly as an ant, smacking his lips for a drink of water, and conducted a census that found while most patrons were white, some were black, Korean, and even—good god!—brown. Silver considered a confrontation with the brown folk, but he kept his hands in his pockets and hummed a few bars of "Cielito Lindo," hoping the tune might get him escorted out. But nothing of the sort occurred. The elderly tourists, it appeared, were hard of hearing.

Silver wet his whistle at a drinking fountain that shot up a spine of water as cold as ice. He promenaded down a wide hallway and put an end to his leisurely stroll to gawk at a larger-than-life portrait of Reagan. Silver focused on the crowd that surrounded the portrait, many of whom were sobbing.

When one gent saluted the portrait, Silver closed his eyes to that ludicrous gesture. But even behind his eyelids, he could still make out Reagan and those whipping flags. He made out the immigrant poor and himself, shoeless and shirtless and thus forbidden service in a Republican county. Silver pictured himself squirting not lighter fluid on those flags but hosing them with high-octane gasoline from a Chevron pump.

Then, as before, he felt a tap on his shoulder. Mrs. Bartlett? Security? When he opened his eyelids, he encountered Amber, his cheerleading poetry student. Her smile was wide and sincere, and troubling to Silver.

"Professor!" Amber screamed.

Silver feared she might chant P-R-O-F-E-S-S-O R, swinging her arms out and about.

"I have a new poem!" she exclaimed. Then, beady-eyed, she examined from a distance his much-punctured head. "I'm glad to see you're not bleeding any more."

Silver recalled that he had last seen her when he was nursing the head wound. At that time, she was in her cheerleading outfit and her pom-poms accessorized nicely with her ample breasts. Presently she was dressed in a pants suit, the lapel holding a pin of the American flag. "Yeah, well, I feel a lot better today." It was true. He hadn't had to apply more than one soaking of alcohol to his head wounds since the day before. Indeed, he realized, more alcohol (he had located Mrs. Bartlett's cooking sherry) had been applied to his mouth during the last twenty-four hours than to his wounds. He could throw back a cordial of sherry right now.

"Did you like my poem?" Amber inquired as she handed him a brochure.

What poem?

Hands on hips, Amber pouted dramatically. "You don't remember!"

Silver had to admit a hole existed in his memory, along with two other holes resulting from things falling on his head. "But I do!" He bowed his head slightly and scratched his scalp, which was oily, he discovered to his embarrassment. He hadn't bathed in a few days and that realization compelled him to step backward, mindful that Amber—she herself was throwing off a nice scent—could gag from his odor. "My memory . . ."

"That's it!" Amber screamed. "Well, it's actually called 'Memories.' I'm working on a new one called 'More Memories.'" Amber's sunny face darkened suddenly behind a cloud of sadness. "My grandmother has Alzheimer's. You probably guessed from my poem." Amber described the care facility where her grandmother lived and that she was still blessed with a good-natured laughter, although Amber and her parents suspected that the grandmother didn't know what she was laughing at except some perpetual joke running inside her head.

Silver nodded and produced an actor's worry line on his brow. He wondered out loud, "What are you doing here?"

"I work here, Professor!" she explained cheerfully. The cloud had disappeared immediately and the glare of her happiness hurt Silver's eyes. "Part time, I mean. After 'W' was elected, I had to do something." She gazed over Silver's bony landscape of his left shoulder in the direction of the Reagan statue. "One day I'll be able to tell my children that I worked here."

Without a crystal ball, Silver could see it coming: she would marry a Dan Quayle and together they would gaze into each other's eyes and see nothing but the red, white, and blue of waving flags.

"And what are *you* doing here?" she asked playfully, hands positioned on her hips, a posture that pushed out her breasts and Silver's eyeballs.

Good question.

Silver stroked his beard as he searched for a snappy answer. But he leveled with Amber. "I'm here with my landlady, Mrs. Bartlett. She's got to pick up something."

Amber clapped her hands. "Oh, she's so adorable! So cute, so warm, plus a donor to the new wing!" Amber reigned in her giddy assessment as her mood darkened once again. Even the costume jewelry of the American flag attached to her lapel darkened. "Poor thing, her husband . . ." Amber bit a fingernail and refused to finish her thought. However, her cheerfulness returned when her name was called over a loudspeaker. She wagged a finger at Silver and warned him that he had better read her poem or she would never speak to him again.

Silver cherished the wag of her lovely bottom, but restrained from staring, his usual response to nice curves. Instead, he flipped through the brochure that read "Millennium Time Capsule 2000 to 2100." According to the pitch, the Ronald Reagan Presidential Foundation offered you and your loved ones the opportunity to bury precious family mementos in a time capsule. The cost was only $250.00 smack-a-roos. Silver fumed. For him, a time capsule burial began with the lowering of his pants and grunting. And it cost nothing. In fact, he believed his time capsule of pudgy stools might benefit the ecology by encouraging healthy poppies and, granted, an array of horrible ragweed, while the Reagan time capsule did nothing but rob citizens of their money.

"¡*Chale!* Forget that!" He crumpled the brochure and let

it fall to the polished floor. However, he picked it up when
he saw Mrs. Bartlett approach with the gentleman he had
seen earlier in tow. The man was struggling to balance a
large item on his shoulder.

"Professor!" Mrs. Bartlett cried. "Professor, can you help us?"

Mrs. Bartlett had purchased a framed and signed portrait
of Ronald Reagan—her third, apparently, for he recalled two
at home—and he was asked to carry it to the car. The man
brought the portrait down from his shoulders, wiped his brow,
and escaped with hardly a good-bye. Silver grimaced. With
the portrait unwrapped, Silver had a face-off with the
president's ruddy mug.

"¡Ay, Chihuahua!" Silver uttered as he gripped the portrait
of the thirty-fifth president.

"Oh, that's Spanish?" Mrs. Bartlett remarked smartly. She
patted her fingertips together and sang, "Goody, goody."

Silver breathed in and out and squared his stance. He lifted
the portrait at once but put it back down. This sucker's heavy,
Silver complained to himself. Still, with Mrs. Bartlett beaming
at his side, he hoisted it onto his shoulder and took one baby
step and then another, then the larger, more manly strides
of a carpenter moving lumber. As he exited the library, the
tourists parted like a Red Sea though some followed on his
heels, nearly tripping him as they crowded his steps. Some
snapped pictures and more than one child blew bubbles that
rose to chest level before falling earthward.

Silver made his way to the entrance, while Mrs. Bartlett
trailed, picking lint from her sweater, oblivious that he was
ready to collapse. He grumbled, sweated, and injured his right
ear when he misjudged a post—the portrait's wooden frame
hurt like hell when it scuffed his skin. Thus, with blood

added to his sweat, what was he but a martyr bearing a cross? "God, that hurts," Silver whined.

Unbeknownst to all, tourists-turned-photographers snapped an unlikely event of a Republican hater holding up a sacred relic, and one old woman broke from the crowd to wipe his brow. But she jumped back when she inadvertently inhaled a whiff of his B.O.—a terrorist group could have used the concoction in his armpits for chemical warfare.

Thus, Silver trudged toward the Lincoln, legs burning, his lungs depleted, and a trickle of blood falling along his neck. When he fell to one knee, the crowd groaned a communal, "Oh." When one man came forth and tried to help him, Silver waved him off with a snarl. He remained on his knee, catching his breath. Finally, after the respite of a long minute, Silver rose unsteadily and carried through the recently re-surfaced parking lot the great communicator, who, these days, had very little to say.

★

Silver drove the Lincoln to a brightly lit Wal-Mart, where he was tempted to dock the beast in a handicapped space (he had the blue placard to flash at the police, plus a bloody ear to prove his point), but opted to drop Mrs. Bartlett in front of the store. He told her that he would join her in a few minutes. Then he parked near the garbage bin, where he ruled out unloading the portrait of Reagan and performing the *jarabe tapatío* on it.

"What am I doing here?" he murmured as he got out of the Lincoln. Had he abandoned his *raza*? His canon of Chicano Zen nothingness? He had just helped carry a portrait of the president that he despised above all others, though Nixon was right up there too, and, hey, there was the gang of two, George and George W. Silver's favorite president was Ulysses S. Grant, a boozer who during his time could hold his own, even on the back of a galloping horse.

He touched his wound, which was little more than a scratch. Still, it spurted a little blood and had him wondering—goofily, he admitted—whether he could earn a purple heart or, at least, a booklet of food stamps. He patted his superficial wound and shrugged his shoulders.

The moon was glaring at him and, in the distance, a weed eater was whipping the holy hell out of raggedy dandelions that had declared their independence by lifting themselves from the soil between cracks in the sidewalk. And was that the sound of children splashing in a wading pool? A garden hose replenishing a kitty dish in the back patio? A drugged robin who had gargled the brew of a fertilized lawn was chirping in an elm. The evening advanced with its cloak of darkness. Gnats and mosquitoes were making a nest in the hair of an old sot asleep in a backyard lounge chair. It was a bucolic evening in the suburbs; the citizens were hunkered around kitchen tables cleaning their guns and keeping abreast by reading brochures on the good work of the NRA.

Silver caught up with Mrs. Bartlett, who had to pick up a prescription. She had stopped to fiddle with the needles of a neglected pine tree.

"It's on sale. What do you think, Professor?" Mrs. Bartlett asked. She pushed her face toward the foliage and sniffed.

Think? The tree resembled a stick in dirt.

Silver chose to bolster the moment with an optimistic tone, seeing that he, on a number of occasions, had gotten his feet stuck in dirt, and with his build—135 pounds, twigs for arms and legs—he too might have been appraised as a stick.

"I think it's the wrong season to plant a tree," answered Silver, promoting himself from a chauffeur to an arborist.

"You're right," Mrs. Bartlett responded. She tugged her purse back onto her arm and, massaging her hip, asked, "Now, why am I here?"

Silver believed that that was his question.

"You said you were going to pick up a prescription," Silver supplied. "Is your leg OK?"

Mrs. Bartlett smiled and thanked Silver. "I hurt my hip years ago. Skiing."

While his landlady walked with a limp up an aisle toward the pharmacy, Silver made a dash to the refrigerated section—he thirstily studied the beers and, ready to splurge, dismissed the cheaper brands, particularly his usual Colt .45, a concoction that rocked you on your ass. He chose a tall Beck's, a stylish import, and was hurrying to the cashier when he was stopped by Jason, his poetry student, who was slapping a small purchase against his palm.

Silver was stymied how to react to this inconvenient encounter. He offered up a simple "Hey."

"Hey," Jason echoed in return.

The two regarded what each held in his paw. Silver had his twenty-four-ounce brew and Jason a pack of form-fitting condoms.

"Who's the gal?" Silver snooped, grinning.

Jason smiled back and revealed the chrome ball on his tongue. "How do you know it's going to be a girl?"

Silver stroked his beard; the kid was a handful. "Yeah, well, enjoy yourself."

"You too," Jason said, lifting his eyebrows at the Beck's beer Silver had moved into the crook of his right arm and cuddled like a baby.

The two got in line, the professor stationed first out of courtesy and social position. Silver fumbled for his wallet, brought out two dollars—he had, by all accounts, four dollars left, except for the two twenties he had snatched from Petersen and hid in his sock for a truly rainy day—and quickly pushed his reservoir of wealth back into his back pocket.

"You need a couple of dollars?" Jason asked.

Silver ignored Jason's snide inquiry and didn't bring his eyes to the cashier's when he displayed his soggy dollars in her outstretched hand. He took his brew in paper, not plastic, and ignored Jason, who said he was working on a new poem. Silver hurried over to Mrs. Bartlett, whom he spotted turning in circles, lost in the fluorescent glare of an overly bright store.

"Mrs. Bartlett," Silver called in a tone of concern. Out of the corner of his eye, he could see Jason approaching from behind and swinging his small package.

Mrs. Bartlett smiled and the apples of her cheek shone red. She limped toward Silver cautiously.

Jason sidled up to the two and, without a word, joined them as they made slow progress through the parking lot to the Lincoln. The young man offered Silver a beckoning gaze that pleaded, "Let me go with you, please." Softhearted, Silver accepted the additional passenger with only a tiny grunt of disapproval. He posted his Beck's between his legs, unopened.

"He's a student of mine," Silver, eyes raised into the rearview mirror, explained to Mrs. Bartlett. "He needs a ride back to campus." He turned to Jason and remarked, "Isn't that right?"

"Mostly."

"That's OK," Mrs. Bartlett said kindly.

Silver pulled out of the parking lot worried. He hoped she hadn't fallen and hurt her hip. He snatched another look in the rearview mirror: Mrs. Bartlett was going through her purse in search of something—she moved her coin purse, her empty amber-colored pill bottles, a white handkerchief, lipstick, a roll of dimes, a roll of Butterscotch Life Savers, the tinkling wind chimes of bobby pins hooked together. She muttered sweetly when Silver banked the Lincoln, the portrait of Reagan on top shifting.

Silver eyed Jason to keep quiet when the young man turned on the radio. In response, Jason turned off the radio and slunk in his seat.

At home, Silver squeezed the Lincoln in the garage, helped Mrs. Bartlett out of the back, and gently led her to the front door, promising not to forget to unload the cargo on top of the car.

"I'll just be a minute," he promised Mrs. Bartlett, whose open purse was hanging on her arm. Silver gently snapped it closed for her.

After she was inside and the front door closed, Silver suggested to Jason, "Let's have a pow-wow." But first Silver pried open his Beck's beer on the door handle of the Lincoln and drank noiselessly three manly swallows. He burped crudely.

The two sat on the lawn still damp from an earlier shower from the sprinklers. The street was dark and grew darker when a porch light went out. A dog barked behind a fence. A car swung around the corner and momentarily lit up their eyeballs. A wind blew, yet neither experienced a nighttime chill.

Silver sipped on his beer. "So who are those for? The dick stockings."

Jason grew sullen and shifted onto his rear end. "I don't know."

Silver permitted the answer to percolate in the part of his brain where answers were deciphered. During his tenure as a hot Chicano lover boy back in the '70s, he had bought condoms weekly and always knew when, where, and with whom he planned to slip on his wet suit and test the depths of pleasure. Kids these days! He took another swig and leaned back on an elbow, getting comfy. He felt comforted that the young man was at least prepared should a young woman tap him on the shoulder and suggest, "Let's play." He told him as much, that and—he took a long swig of his brew—what the fuck was wrong with him?

"I don't know."

There it was again, an answer that held no meaning. The sky spit a shooting star, and Silver was slow in raising a hand and saying, "Hey, did you see that?" But he had much more to talk about than stars that fall and burn, like people. Instead, he pried: "You're rich."

"My dad's rich, my grandfather's real rich."

"Then you're rich too."

Jason pulled up his socks, as if he were getting ready to go. "I can't help it."

The silence between then rose like the moon. And under the moon of their suspicions, they grew closer, Silver charitably allowing the young man to chug on his Beck's. But Silver was watchful of his suds. Hell, he had only one tall one and didn't mean to give away more than a few ounces of a fine German brew. He nearly pulled it out of Jason's mouth when he took a second chug. But Silver checked himself and, in the dark, he weighed Jason's ambition to write poetry and experience a world outside of Simi Valley.

"Why don't you come with me to Oakland?" Silver could

have thunked the beer bottle over his own head. Why did he say that?

Jason sat up, his eyes bright under the moon. "Can I?"

A single-engine plane, with two red lights pulsating on its wings, cut across the night sky. An owl hooted in a far tree, where abandoned nests were threatened to unravel before a strong wind. A porch light came on and a man appeared, calling his dog. Such was the commotion of a suburb with money.

"Yeah, if you leave your money home," Silver finally answered. He didn't know why he would make that part of the bargain. Hell, if he was going to have a kid hanging around him, he would prefer to have one with dollars in his pockets.

"You really want to write?" Silver asked.

"Yeah."

"Listen, man, you got to respond better than 'Yeah.'" Silver sucked the last suds of his Beck's and placed the mouth of the bottle to his ear, listening to the sound of a howling ocean mad about one thing or another.

"What should I say?" Jason asked.

"You're the poet, dude. What do you think you should say?"

When Jason didn't offer a response immediately, he handed the empty Beck's bottle to Jason. "What do you hear?"

Jason, head tilted, listened to the sound in wonderment. "I hear the sea."

"How is it? What's its mood? Like canned laughter or what?"

The roar of a jet from Burbank forced them into silence. By the time the jet had passed, taking with it its light and noise, Jason had an eye peering inside the mouth of the bottle. He sniffed the end and then put the end to his ear again.

"This is not a multiple choice, Holmes. Give me an answer!"

"It's like it's angry or something."

Silver clapped once. "There you go, *carnal!* The sea's pissed off and it's going to roll over us when the glaciers all melt. It's going to carry away your grandfather and your father and all our dirty butts, *también.*"

"Cool," Jason remarked. His face widened with happiness. "And all their money is going to float away!"

"*¡Eso!*"

Silver hated to see the happiness slide off Jason's face. But he asked about his grandfather, founder of Simi Valley College, and Jason just answered that his grandfather was an immensely rich born-again Christian. His money had come from real estate, and oil, Jason said, the sweat of others.

"*Eso,*" Silver crowed. "Now that's how a poet thinks. "'The sweat of others.' Just remember that."

Thus they got to know each other and sparked up a bent joint pulled from Jason's hip pocket—the scent of *mota* sweetened the lawn as the night sky spit shooting stars. They smoked and laughed, and on their knees caravanned across the lawn, where they lowered their faces to drink from a dribbling sprinkler head. The water was sweet, clean, and free. They laughed until they were on their backs.

"Help me," Silver finally said after the giggles subsided. He got to his wobbly feet.

They weighed each other's strength when they undid the portrait of Reagan from the car roof, balanced it awkwardly in their light buzz, and leaned it against a wall in the living room. They returned outside and pulled their muscles together to lift the cast-iron statue of the red-lipped Negro boy holding up a shoe.

"Now this thing we got in our arms is past tense," Silver stated.

"Past tense," repeated Jason, goofy on *mota*. He giggled and said that he craved another drink from the sprinkler head.

"Nah, man, another day. We got to correct the politics of this place!" Silver smacked his lips, dry as twigs from the shared joint. He could have kicked himself for not buying a whole six-pack: the mouths of empty beer bottles would roar a mighty ocean.

They lugged the statue halfway up the street and stopped once to adjust the weight in their hands, as if they were gripping Southern history that had to be taken to the dump. During the rest, Silver asked, "Jason, you know Professor Petersen?"

Jason shook his head. "Nah, but he's an asshole." Jason giggled and dropped his end of the statue. Tears of pleasure leaked from his eyes, and his nose ran.

They deposited it in the privet hedge.

They returned to Mrs. Bartlett's front lawn, where they lay, arms behind their backs, and watched planes and shooting stars. But as the dew began to rise from the grass and his buzz began to recede, Silver sat up and told Jason that he had to go in. He had observed the shadow of Mrs. Bartlett pass, then darkness envelop the house as she snapped off the lamps one after another.

"You sure you don't know Petersen?" Silver intended to gather as much information as he could about a professor who dealt drugs on the side.

"No, I just know him from when I see him." Jason's own buzz had come to an abrupt end. He appeared sad, and he shared his sadness with Silver, who was now raking the itch of grass from his back—he had taken off his sweatshirt.

Silver probed. "So who's this girl of yours?"

Jason released a sigh and looked away, as if someone had called him.

"You don't want to talk about it?"

Jason shook his head. Then, after a plane passed and the night sky spat three more falling stars, he volunteered cryptically. "You know who she is."

Silver was reaching for a stalk of grass stuck to his shoulder. "Nah, Homes, I don't know who she is." He fit the stalk into his mouth, half expecting to taste the salt that had washed up from his running spurts throughout the day.

"She's Wesley and Laura's daughter. She's away at college back East."

Silver spit out the stalk, for he was tasting not salt but something closer to the grit of fertilized earth.

★

Silver assumed dreams were weightless, but he felt the air from his lungs escape in a rush that had the scent of beer, *mota*, and his last meal of turkey sandwich. And he was certain that dreams were also black and white, and maybe red if a person had been drinking hard liquor. But in this dream he saw sparks of green, blue, bright pink, and bronze. When his peepholes became unglued from sleep, he made out in the dark two nipples descending toward his face. What was in the joint he and Jason shared? He shouldn't have drunk like a dog from the sprinkler head—maybe he had the first signs of hoof and mouth disease.

"Ah," he bellowed. His face became smothered by a bad dream.

"Do you like it?" the voice asked after the breasts backed away.

Dreams talk?

He managed to roll from his back to his stomach and place a pillow over his head. But the pillow was yanked off. The dream faded when he felt the skin on his neck lift from a suctioning kiss. Laura announced in a whisper, "I'm washed."

"What are you doing?"

Laura had no time for small talk but let Silver be on top for a change. Ten minutes later, he lay exhausted when it was over. He rolled onto his back and stroked her hair. In turn, she stroked his beard.

"Laura, how did you get here?" He had noticed that the screen window was pushed aside. Had she been trolling for Chicano flesh?

"Silver, you sure don't know your geography." She told him that she lived only a block away.

"You walked here in your nightie?" He pictured her ghosting through the neighborhood, the speechless cats following her odyssey as she stepped over damp lawns and flowerbeds and jumped one or two fences. "Won't Wesley find out?"

"He's asleep, silly."

Silver risked asking why she suddenly wanted to see him. Didn't she call off their relationship?

"Oh, mama missed you so much." She raised her left breast—the one he was partial to—and he suctioned its nub until he felt a burp rise in his throat.

"Nice baby," Laura remarked. "Baby likes to sleep with mama, huh?"

Laura seemed in a jolly mood, her belly rolling with laughter when Silver farted after she leaned an elbow on his stomach. When she began to cry, Silver was surprised by the hotness of the tears.

"What's wrong?" he asked.

"Everything."

Silver stroked her hair, cuddled her. "Like what?"

Her crying rocked her shoulders and belly, and with Silver attached to her in a hug, he rode out the vibrations of her sadness.

"I don't want to be married. I want to be free."

Free?

"I missed out," she sobbed. "You had all the fun, I didn't. Everyone had fun but me."

Was being homeless all the fun? Missed meals? Road camp with certified alcoholics and mean husbands who took out their anger on the weeds they whacked from roadsides?

She pushed away from Silver and said, "Taste my tears."

Silver's tongue licked up the runoff.

"What do you taste?"

Silver shrugged. "Nothing, really."

She cried. "See, I'm not even salty." She wiped away her tears. "I'm married to a good but boring old man." She hugged Silver, and cried until his shoulder was wet. "I want to do something!"

Silver began to play with himself slowly, but really went to town when he gauged that a smile cut into her cheeks. When his member was presentable, he nudged her hefty legs apart, positioned his flesh in the gash of her sex, and, as lead oarsman on a slave ship, began rowing again.

"Come on, ensign," she moaned playfully, "I missed you. I know that you didn't miss me, but I don't care."

He put a little more push to her pull, but soon tired. She pulled off the bed sheet and flopped him on his back.

"I'll you show you how it's done!" she said gleefully.

"Be gentle," Silver said seriously.

"Take it like a man!" she laughed.

With the moon of her bottom glowing from the real moonlight that flowed through the window, she rose and fell robustly on his rudder. If the sheet had been wrapped around her, it would have filled like a sail and moved the bed across the bedroom.

He was tired, raw down there. He was in a rush to get his lover off him—there must be a clause in the rental contract about nighttime visitors, he figured. He tapped her bottom and interrupted her by calling, "Laura, I have something to ask you."

She turned and asked tenderly, "What, lover boy?"

He wanted to ask about her daughter, but he saw a pleasure on her face that was part of his doing. His curiosity dissipated. Instead, he thought he would stroke her confidence. "Laura, you're doing a really good job."

She slapped his spindly thigh playfully and proceeded to bounce on the poet, who turned his gaze from her moonlit bottom to the blackness of the ceiling.

Chapter Ten

Silver woke with the bruises from a fitful sleep under his eyes. He sat at the edge of his bed and scrubbed them with his fists, but they wouldn't come clean. He rolled back into bed and asked, what did I just do? Then he remembered. Laura had climbed into his window, made love to him, and cried that her life was empty. To make her feel better, he told her that his life was as empty as hers. This only had her sobbing into his pillow.

"She wants to be Chicana," Silver told himself. She was tired of her role as the wife of a Baptist college president and petitioned Silver to introduce her to her Hispanic heritage. That part of the evening was clear. When he argued that you couldn't take classes to be Chicano, that you had to be born into that brownness in which nothing good or easy would come your way, Laura poked his throat with her lacquered hairdo and squeezed him into a headlock until Silver's tongue lolled like a snake escaping from outside his mouth. She demanded more from life, something he was born with—a Chicano soul, for Christ's sake!

"OK, OK," he begged in her grip. He hurt mightily. He massaged his neck, a pipeline that connected his brain to his body and washed all its tissues with his blood. Since he was without health insurance, he wondered if he, as a person used to getting by with only Band-Aids and aspirin, could possibly use a toilet roll for a neck brace.

Laura cooed in his ear that he was a darling, smooched

his neck to make it better, and stuck her head under the covers and journeyed down. And while she was down, Silver prayed to the Christian and non-Christian gods that he could talk her into driving him—and Jason, his protégé—to East Los Angeles, where he could catch a bus back to Oakland. He had to make a move.

"*Ay, Dios,*" he groaned as Laura attached herself.

Silver saw his forty-one years pass before him. He had faced gunfire, knives, thugs of all shades, insane roosters, rookie cop, drunks, and pit bulls that bounded over chain-link fences. Then there were those middle-class relatives who argued convincingly that he was lazy, citing his one pair of shoes—beat-up huaraches—that only the poorest of the poor in Mexico would wear. Words and opinions hurt, deflating his worth. But he was never so frightened as he was at the moment with Laura's mouth around his thing.

After she was done, he remembered her daughter, Jenny, and was of the opinion that since he was Jason's poetry teacher he had a right to inquire about her whereabouts. But, as he was scared of Laura, he held his tongue. He just lay next to her, watching her fall asleep, though occasionally a sob would shake her shoulders. She was upset about missing something, like the love of a strong Chicano perhaps.

So much for the evening. When he was finally awake, the western wall was feathered with morning sunlight. He got up, peeled the residue of a nightmare from the corners of his eyes, and scratched at the bloodstained pillow. Was Laura that on hard me? he mused. But he quickly accounted for the source of that stain. It was from the frame of Reagan's portrait that had clipped his ear. There was no argument that he had bled for a president. He chuckled, but stopped when his head began to throb with pain.

He padded down the hall, dressed in a fresh set of clothes that he had found on a chair.

"Mrs. Bartlett," he hailed softly. His stomach rumbled for eggs, poached, scrambled, or raw as his eyes. He could do with a plate of *frijoles* and a tortilla, and the hot brew of designer coffee, though the regular grog of instant coffee would suffice. Or if only he could sniff around a glazed maple bar before his teeth calibrated the size and width of that empty-calorie pastry and got to work.

She wasn't in the kitchen and she wasn't in the living room. Her knitting was on the couch and the portrait of Reagan right where he had left it. He then recalled her ailment of a sore hip.

"Mrs. Bartlett," he called, "I'm up. Are you OK?" The house was silent, except the swinging eyes of the owl clock in the kitchen. Was she ill? He was nervous that he would be forced to call the paramedics. But a sound drew him to the front door, which was ajar.

When Silver peeked out, he saw a sunny Mrs. Bartlett pointing at an area roped with police yellow caution tape— an arena that contained his Beck's beer bottle. A cop with latex gloves enveloping his meaty hands was bending to pick it up.

"*Chingao,*" Silver whispered. He shuffled backward, picking up static that raised his beard into the makings of a tumbleweed. All that police work for a single beer bottle? Then he recalled that he and Jason, suddenly activists with a revolutionary political agenda, had ejected the cast-iron statue from the neighborhood. And was that their burnt doobie on the lawn? Would the twigs of two burnt matches be counted as evidence?

Silver scampered back to his bedroom, slipped into his huaraches, and hurried into the bathroom, where he splashed his face and drank like a camel, as it was clear that the day would be long. He sneaked out the back door and jumped the fence, coming down with a grunt that buckled his gimpy knees. A sleuth, he scrutinized the wide footsteps of Laura's own trek. Would the police make something of her prints, too?

Silver returned to campus and to his office—he had forgotten his keys and had a janitor open it for him. He sat in the squeaky prof's chair and permitted sweat to glaze his body, as he was too tired to blot his chest and armpits with what was handy, namely a ream of typing paper. He would take a shower in the gym at first convenience.

He was going through a drawer for chewing gum—he hadn't brushed his teeth—when the telephone began to ring. Silver stared at it. The call could be from anyone, maybe even god, who was having a good laugh in the comedy lounge up in heaven. He reached for it.

"Yeah," Silver said hesitantly.

"Fuck you!" the voice snarled. It was the little man in the black suit greeting him in the only way he knew. He giggled and said after a few snorts of laughter, "Professor, I'm sorry for what happened the other day."

Silver stood up, growled, and got to the point: "I don't deal drugs, turd face!" Silver took note that his use of profanity had increased since he had arrived in Blanche.

"What kind of talk is that from a professor?" the little man questioned with a lilt to his voice. He appeared to be enjoying himself. "Your buddy, the one who is enjoying what you call it?"

"Sabbatical."

"Yeah, that scam. Petersen, or the guy who flies for Petersen. He never picked up the job. Where the fuck he is, we don't care. We're not really out of anything. A new order is on its way through another supplier."

Silver predicted that soon all the rich noses of Blanche would be rung with a light powdering of cocaine. More than one housewife would be subdued in front of her television set, a wreath of marijuana smoke around her pretty neck. Soon the citizens would be giggling in backyards, where their pools reflected sky and an occasional bird got drunk on the fertilizer laced in flowerbeds.

"Then why are you calling me?"

The little man giggled. "I thought I should tell you."

"Tell me what?"

"I'm going to kill you just because."

Silver hung up, spooked. He bit a fingernail and sensed the rising tide of nervousness in his armpits.

The telephone immediately rang again. Silver stared at it wearily. Maybe this time it was god calling. Maybe god had a knock-knock joke to share with the less fortunate. When he picked it up, Silver discovered the voice belonged to Petersen.

"It's cool, amigo" Petersen said lightly. He sounded chipper.

"What are you talking about?" Silver asked roughly.

Petersen brought him up to date about his pilot buddy, whose flying fortress had apparently not picked up the drugs. In short, they weren't responsible for not delivering. But his buddy was missing—his plane was lost in the Bermuda Triangle for all he knew, for all he cared. Chuckling, Petersen also theorized that his buddy might have taken off to Mexico for a private matter that involved a woman on the side.

Silver halted the narrative about the friend and the friend's girlfriend and scolded, "Fuck you, Petersen!" He hung up, then picked up the receiver and let it buzz. He didn't want to hear from anyone.

When the fax machine started up, Silver jumped. Scared, he didn't recognize the sound of the machine at first. People are trying to reach me any which way, he thought. But as the fax machine scrolled its diplomalike paper, he saw that it was a communication from Tyronne, who held down the headquarters of their two-bedroom bungalow in Oakland. Silver tore it out of the machine and read: "Your momma called yesterday right after 'Wheel of Fortune' and axed what the fuck happened to the jumper cables? She says on top of no Christmas presents you ain't going get no birthday present neither. Says you one lazy dog." He ended by asking where in the hell was his money Silver had promised.

Silver crumpled up the message and shot it at the wastebasket. He was angry because he was painfully aware of what had become of the jumper cables: he had lent them to another buddy to jump-start his old American Pacer with the fish-bowl windshield. He got it started, but was arrested two blocks later for littering—a bumper had fallen off in the road—and for driving with a suspended license. As the cherries of the police cruiser came on, his friend added to the commotion by chucking beer cans and wine bottles from the floorboard. It didn't help things when he got out of the car and shouted to the police, "Do I look like I smoke marijuaña?" His bronze belt buckle held the shape of a marijuana leaf.

Silver was hurt by his mother's scolding. True, he seldom listened to her, and when he did, the result was he often had a job that bored him silly. Silver assessed his mother's meanness: he didn't mind not receiving Christmas presents, but no more birthday presents ever again! She really knew how to hurt a son.

He should later replace those jumper cables and the hedge clippers, and prove to his sourpuss of a mother that he was not a lazy soul. To do this, he had to claim his paycheck. He put the receiver back into the cradle of the telephone. He breathed in and out, and braved a chitchat with Mildred.

"Office of the president," Mildred stated bureaucratically.

"Millie, it's me."

Mildred hung up violently.

With a finger, Silver plumbed the hurt and waxy cavern of his ear. He evaluated his error in calling Mildred Millie, a name reserved for mules and horses, she had repeatedly told him. He risked a second call. To protect himself, he placed the phone to his undamaged ear, and appropriately a foot away. He also tried a different tactic when Mildred answered: he deepened his voice, which he believed improved his stature or, at least, made him sound like a black disc jockey. He bellowed: "This is Professor Mendez calling on a matter of some urgency." His heart beat as he expected her to hang up even more roughly.

"Yes, Professor." Mildred was breathing icicles. They evaporated when he lied that he had read her poetry and admired it enormously. She softened. "Yes, what is it?"

If Silver had sported a tail instead of a few renegade tufts of hair, it would have begun to wag. He liked his luck and squeaked, "Hey, is my check in?"

"'Hay' is for horses, Professor," said Mildred sharply. The icicles had re-formed. "And, in the future, please remember I'm not a Millie."

If Silver ever saw President Skaggs again he would defi-
nitely suggest anger-management classes for her. For the time
being, he opted to remain civil. "I'm sorry, MIL-DRED." He
swallowed. "Well, is it in?"

Mildred notified him that she had sent it to his home.

"What?" Silver screamed. He envisioned Tyronne opening
his mail with a long, yellow fingernail and grinning at the
watermark on the back of the check as he held it up to the
light. On the kitchen counter, cluttered with dirty dishes,
he would endorse the back "Silvestre Mendez" in the scrawl
of a high school dropout. He envisioned Tyronne eating a
bag of barbecue potato chips while sprinting down to the
check-cashing service around the corner. Silver had used the
service on repeated occasions and had added his own DNA
to the plate glass smeared with the fingerprints of other desperate people.

"Don't you yell at me!" Mildred snapped.

Silver reigned in his anger. "I'm sorry."

"I sent it two days ago. Ask your landlady."

Silver sighed. The check hadn't gone to Oakland after
all, but to Mrs. Bartlett's. He hung up while Mildred was
telling him that President Skaggs was looking for him to
complete the school poem he had requested at the beginning
of the semester.

"Shit," Silver muttered, then went mute. He looked up
at the poster of Walt Whitman, then James Joyce. Both were
dead and yet had more to say than Silver at the moment.
Finally, he pushed himself out of his chair.

"It ain't over," Silver predicted confidently.

He showered at the gym, gargling like a bird and brushing
his teeth with fingernails serrated from his nervous chewing

during the last two days. He left the campus none too soon—
President Skaggs was walking with Laura toward the library.
Laura was a few feet in front of her husband, her high
heels chipping the sidewalk under the weight of her quick,
seemingly angry, steps. Silver mustered up a tenderness for
Wesley, a poor, defenseless man against her demands for this
or that. He was curious about Jenny, their daughter. Where
did she go? Why hadn't Laura mentioned her? Had she escaped
her parents and, in turn, a Baptist life?

He put his legs into action and returned to his landlady's,
nearly tiptoeing as he got closer to the house. He was on
high alert for police, even sniffing for the scent of donuts.
The once quarantined lawn presently held an audience of
pecking birds. He lamented the evening, during which time
he invited Jason to join him in Oakland. He prayed the kid
would forget.

Silver jumped when the dog he had rescued barked. The
pooch beckoned Silver by scratching at a gate, like a furry
convict.

"Hang in there, dude," Silver told the dog, who had put a
paw between the slats, an appeal for dog and man to shake
and be friends. Silver couldn't resist the tender gesture; he
hurried over and shook the dog's paw and reiterated: "Hang
in there, dude." He stroked the dog's snout and didn't recoil
when the dog's tongue rolled from his mouth and licked
Silver's fingers.

He debated whether to knock or just walk in after a light
brush of his huaraches on the "Jesus Loves You" mat. The
debate ended when the door opened and a woman greeted
him with a friendly, "You must be Professor Mendez." She
was in her early forties, Silver's age, but unlike Silver, nicely

dressed, smooth as porcelain in face and neck, and smelling of flowers and clean hundred-dollar bills. Her blue eyes were clear, while Silver's eyes were jammed with the traffic of red veins. Her hair was arranged nicely and Silver's hair was stringy from his shower at the gym. He wondered shamefully if the scabs on his scalp showed.

"That's right," Silver said weakly. He had gotten used to the title of Professor, though he acknowledged it had yet to exercise any influence over the people in Blanche, except at his poetry reading, where static electrified the air. Silver, however, was unaware of his influence on campus. Little did he know that a few men were letting their facial hair grow with the intention of producing lightning from their whiskers. One of the braver men had taken to wearing huaraches and another, still braver, had begun to fast in imitation of Silver's leanness—it was rumored that Silver lived on only one meal a day, but that piece of campus mythology was an exaggeration. Sometimes the mysterious professor didn't bring anything to his lips for the day but his salty knuckle on which to suck while he reviewed the state of his poverty.

"I'm Helen's daughter, Carolyn." She extended a hand that was soft as a dove.

Silver took her hand gently. He muttered, "Hello," followed by, "Is it OK if I come in?"

"Of course!" she answered gleefully.

Silver self-consciously stepped inside the house. On the living room wall already hung, albeit slightly askew, the Ronald Reagan portrait purchased the day before.

"Where's Mrs. Bartlett?" Silver asked.

Carolyn became silent.

"What happened? Is she OK?" Silver worried that she had

a heart attack seconds after one of the police officers informed her that a doobie had been found snubbed on the front lawn. He sensed the effervescence of poetry bubbling up inside him—or was it dizziness from not having eaten?—as he pictured a friend of hers writing her obituary at a kitchen table. Her friend was stating for public record how tasty the crust of Mrs. Bartlett's apple pie was. The pie would be sorely missed, and so would the deceased.

"My mother's hip is bothering her again, and she's going to stay with us for a few days."

Silver constructed a worried look. He asked if she had overexerted herself when the two of them had gone to the Reagan library the day before.

"No, it's just an old injury." She fretted for a moment, but realizing that she had a guest brightened and beckoned for Silver to have a seat as she led him to the couch. She crossed her arms across her breasts and bit her lower lip before saying, "I know mother liked your company. But with her gone, do you . . ."

Silver could see it coming and helped her out. "Actually, I found a new place. That's why I left early this morning." He mused whether Blanche had a Rescue Mission, where he could bed down for the evening. "I'm just back—" He cut his eyes to a pile of mail on the coffee table in front of the couch. He fought the urge to reach over and rifle through the pile. So he coolly stated: "I was expecting a letter."

Carolyn appeared confused.

Silver pointed at the mail stacked on the table.

"Oh, of course. Please take a look."

Silver leaned over and began to sort through the mail. His jaw weakened. His beard nearly lifted as he sorted through one letter after another from the Republican Party and two from the Reagan library. There was a letter from George Bush's Points of Light Foundation and the American Federation of Over-Taxed Southern California Home Owners. It appeared that Mrs. Bartlett was a soft touch, and her house was a frequent target for Republican fund-raising.

He finally located the check from Simi Valley Baptist College. Instead of ripping it open and gloating over the amount, he stood up and placed it in his back pocket.

"Professor, there's something else."

Silver remained standing.

"Someone stole mother's statue and—"

"I thought I heard something last night." His armpits began to churn out sweat, salt, and—Silver's nose wiggled— the stew of B.O. "And I thought we were living in a safe area!"

"Well, that's part of it." Carolyn hesitated as she rotated her wedding ring so that the rock no longer showed its brilliance. "There were also drugs."

Silver could make out the faucet drips in the kitchen and the tick of the owl-shaped clock with swinging eyes. The house creaked, though there was no footfall or wind outside to push against its four corners. And was that his newly found dog whimpering in the yard? He looked about suspiciously, took three quiet steps, and listened. He had a premonition that the police would appear from around the door, and, indeed, a plain-clothes detective did appear. His coat was unbuttoned, exposing a blue tie draped over a slight paunch.

Silver's instinct was to throw his hands into the air. Instead, he offered a weak "hello" to the detective, who buttoned his jacket, a gesture that inferred to Silver that the officer had been expecting a tousle. But after one glance at Silver, he had apparently taken the high opinion that he could squish Silver with his pinkie.

"This is Detective Ford," Carolyn said.

Silver's attention was drawn to the Reagan portrait, the great communicator, who was at present telling him, as he was telling himself, "Buster, your days are numbered."

The detective questioned Silver about the stolen statue, and Silver, once again seated on the couch, knees pressed together, made a hundred faces of shock, remarking how scandalous the youth of the time were pulling all sorts of pranks. The detective reported that drugs were involved—they had recovered a spent doobie—and implied that he had it in mind to have it tested for DNA. With that, Silver pressured his face to make more outraged faces, again blaming youth, the oppressive Catholic Church (to Silver, the detective appeared a Catholic-hater), and every country in South America.

"Colombia is such a backward country!" Silver exclaimed.

"My grandmother is from Colombia," Detective Ford retorted.

Silver melted and played with his fingers.

The detective laughed and said, "Hell, no, my grandmother's not from Colombia, she's from Bakersfield." He laughed openly at Silver, and Carolyn put on a smile, then excused herself when the telephone rang in the kitchen.

The detective wiped a bloated tear from his eye. His smile collapsed. "You're from Mexico, huh?"

Silver shook his head.

"Mexico's got a drug problem, huh?"

Silver toughened. "Nah, the pharmaceuticals got a problem. Selling overpriced pills. Even condoms I hear cost more than they used to."

"My wife's a pharmacist." His hands were now on his hips, exposing the badge on his belt.

Silver suspected that the detective was pulling his leg, like his grandmother being from Colombia. But the crooked line that was his mouth remained crooked, and mean.

"Yeah, well, I hear that they get pretty good pay. Pharmacists, you know."

Silver admonished himself for his cowardliness. But he was tired of Blanche and all of Simi Valley. He just wanted to get out and fast. In fact, Silver became aware that he was seated on the portion of the couch with the hydraulic lift. In spite of his reduced stature as a suspected criminal, he had to joke in his mind whether there were speeds to the couch's ejection. Perhaps if he flew into the air, he could be out the back door before the officer could uncurl his pinkie.

"We don't want drugs in our community," Detective Ford stated firmly.

Silver agreed with a shake of his head.

"We have a clean community."

"Yeah, I noticed there was hardly no litter at all."

Detective Ford scowled.

"This is not a joking matter, Mendez." He hiked up his pants and reddened in the face. Fists closed, he was striding toward Silver when Carolyn returned from the kitchen.

"Is that your dog in the yard?" Carolyn asked.

Silver was glad for her reappearance. Yes, he admitted, and said that he had befriended the pooch and that he had received Mrs. Bartlett's permission, even encouragement, to keep the dog. If he had been Pinocchio, his nose could have held a nation of sparrows. He was making things up as he went along, and Detective Ford suspected as much.

"I have to go," the detective said to Carolyn. "You have my card and, don't worry, we'll patrol the street regularly." He then eyed Silver. "May I talk to you?"

Silver followed the detective into the hallway.

"Stay away from Jason," Detective Ford whispered, tapping Silver's breastbone. "His grandfather doesn't like your kind."

"You mean . . . poets?" Silver inquired.

"Nah, Mendez, your kind."

Silver understood clearly when the detective glared at Silver's huaraches and asked how come he didn't wear athletic shoes like everybody else. He pulled not-so-gently on Silver's beard and growled, "What's this all about?"

Silver refused to answer. He stepped back into the living room even after the detective asked him to come back, that he wasn't done. Silver thought: "Eat shit!"

After the detective left, once again promising Carolyn that they would get to the bottom of the statue's disappearance and again reminding him that the police would patrol the street, Silver rushed to the kitchen for a glass of water. He was filling up, he the camel with miles to trudge through the blinding light of a Republican county.

Chapter Eleven

Silver admired the dog's skipping step as well as his initiative to lead the way down the leafy street, which had a neighbor poking his head from the raised hood of his American car, a dipstick in hand. Silver was too troubled by Detective Ford's indirect threats to make it on his own. He was glad for the companionship of a dog, and the dog, though feisty after a day of R & R in Mrs. Bartlett's backyard, took the journey slow. Lucky for Silver. The sun had climbed above the trees, and the heat of the day had slowed his stride.

"I'm going to call you Baloney," Silver told the dog. He was impressed with the dog's ability to nibble those nitrate-laced slices with better manners than most people, including himself. He could also see that once filled out he would be shaped like a cylindrical length of baloney.

Baloney stopped to lick wet lawns, raise a leg against a tree but shoot nothing, and bite the fur under his left front leg for fleas. Silver required those little rests, but broke into a trot when he saw Detective Ford pass in a white cruiser, mouthing something through his closed window. Silver believed it was "Wetback." A German Shepherd sat in the back seat. Yawning, the dog displayed a strap of purplish tongue and teeth embedded, Silver was convinced, with Mexican flesh.

"Come on, little dude," he called after Baloney. He whistled for the dog to get his short wheels spinning.

They hurried two blocks without glancing back. Silver seldom drew guidance from the Bible but recalled a woman who looked back and turned into a pillar of salt. Silver had a premonition that that might happen to him. He would dissolve into salt and the neighbors would rush over with pails. Come spring, they would use his remains to battle an armada of slugs heading for flowerbeds.

They quickly put five blocks between Mrs. Bartlett's home and where they now rested under the canopy of an elm tree. A nest pitched precariously in the crooks of the limbs was abandoned, the tiny birds having flown the coop. He had dropped the plastic garbage bag of his possessions, clothes mainly, but also a comb, a map of the Los Angeles area, and a hard-bristled toothbrush for scrubbing his teeth and raking his tongue clean of all the profanity that it uttered daily.

Silver had to concede that he had had enough, and with the check in his back pocket, soon to be moved inside one of his huaraches, a secret hiding place no one with a sense of smell would venture, he could return to Oakland a victor! Let the college hunt him down for abandoning his duty as a professor. Fuck them. He mulled over his time at the college and what he could remember of it: he taught on Tuesday and Thursday, and now it was Friday morning. His next class wasn't until next week. Perhaps the students, the five of them all with names like Amber and Jason, wouldn't say anything about their professor's absence. Maybe they would just come to class to sleep and Petersen at the last moment would hear of Silver's absence and assign their grades for the semester. Maybe the college would just learn never to hire a bearded poet.

"Let's go!" Silver yelled at Baloney.

They migrated toward a freeway onramp, where Silver, a geographer of quick departures, anticipated his next move:

he would lick his thumb to see which way the wind blew. Invariably it would blow toward the San Joaquin Valley in the direction of Oakland. But no sooner had he picked up the roar of distant freeway traffic than Petersen pulled up next to them. Petersen was wearing his hat with the lures. His smile was a lure, too.

Good god! thought Silver. Violence boiled in his blood.

"How's it going?" Petersen asked.

"Can't complain," Silver lied. "Just out for a stroll." His strides lengthened and his anger grew. "Asshole."

"Don't be like that."

"Fuck you."

"Get in. Let's be friends. I got something to ask you." Petersen's head, shoulders, and a good portion of his torso leaned out of the car window.

"Why should I?" The answer arrived quickly. Out of the corner of his eye, he glimpsed Laura's Volvo approaching, and right behind her Detective Ford's cruiser. Silver didn't have to be asked a second time. He lifted the garbage bag of his personal things and whistled for Baloney to lower his leg from a rose bush and get in the car.

Petersen drove away and didn't say anything, aside from "temper, temper" when Silver plucked the hat off his head and threw it in the back seat.

"How come you dress like a chump?" Silver asked angrily.

"Disguise."

Silver grumbled. Through the small mirror on his visor, he caught sight of Laura. Her eyes were bitter as almonds, and she was screaming something impolite but protected under the First Amendment.

"Can't you put a little *pedo* to your car, get it going

faster?" Silver begged as he turned back around and gave his attention to Petersen, whose eyes were raised into the rearview mirror.

"Isn't that Mrs. Skaggs behind us?" Petersen asked. When Silver didn't admit as much, he propositioned Silver with a job offer that would put a roof over his head.

Silver remained quiet for two blocks until he couldn't help himself. "What kind of job?"

Petersen reached into the backseat and lifted a duffel bag into the front seat next to Baloney, who sniffed it once and then lowered his head onto his paws. "Open it."

Silver stared at the bag.

"Come on, open it!"

Silver was scared that if he plunged his hand into the bag, his fingers could be bloodied by lures, fish hooks, a gutting knife, or the heads of decapitated catfish. "What you got in there?"

"The remains of Edgar Allen Poe." Petersen laughed and petted Baloney.

Spooky, Silver thought. And to think he was in the front seat with such a lunatic. Did all English profs talk like this after twenty years of teaching poetry? Slowly, Silver unzipped the bag, because for all he knew Petersen could be a serial killer of small people. But there were no dwarf body parts, only small plastic bags of cocaine. "Bastard!"

"I need your help," Petersen pleaded with a smirk. "Come on! I helped you get your teaching job. Now you can help me!"

Silver examined Petersen, whose nostrils were crusted with white powder. His eyes were large and dilated. His hands were jittery on the steering wheel. No wonder his bravado—the guy was tripping on his own product. The other day he wimped out at Denny's, nearly cried when Silver took his wallet and helped himself to some unearned money. Currently he was driving around Blanche with a duffel bag, making deliveries.

As the car pulled up to a red light, Silver clutched his plastic garbage bag of his belongings and whistled for Baloney to jump. Petersen yelled for Silver to be reasonable, but Silver waved him off. He dashed to Laura's Volvo before the light turned green.

"Why are you with him? He's a fool!" Laura roared over the air conditioning.

Silver gripped the seat as Laura put her weight on the gas pedal. With the car rushing to fifty, he reviewed his life as it passed before him, beginning with the people—students and faculty mainly—he had encountered during the last four days. Is that how death comes? You see your life unroll, beginning with the most recent days? This notion was confirmed by the appearance of Jason, propelling himself on his skateboard—in the direction of Mrs. Bartlett's house? He felt sorry for the young man, his protégé, who would knock and find no one at home. Hell, he felt sorry for himself.

"What are you looking at?" Laura viewed the neighborhood outside her window. "Oh, him, that rich little brat! He's nothing but trouble!" She next aimed her vengeance at Baloney, who had pulled in his tongue and shut his trap and curled up politely at Silver's huaraches. "Where did you get this dirty thing?"

Silver ignored her description of the dog he was growing fond of. Instead, he peered over his shoulder—he didn't turn into a pillar of salt after all—and caught sight of Detective Ford pacing their exit from Blanche. Silver was no lip reader, but thought he made out the complete sentence: "Get your wetback ass out of town." The German Shepherd, who had climbed in the front seat, was saying something, too. Silver would have asked Baloney to decipher for him, except his buddy was busily gnawing a flea in his coat. Whatever it was, he knew it wasn't nice.

★

Forty minutes later, Laura's mood changed when she changed lanes to the Atlantic Boulevard exit and pulled slowly into East Los Angeles. She became happy and rolled her window down.

"Ah, the culture," she remarked as she drove slowly down Cesar Chavez Boulevard and viewed two kids straddling low-rider bikes spitting sunflower seed shells at each other. A dog stood between them sniffing the shells. Laura waved at them and waved at three shirtless young men on the primered car fender of a '63 Bel Aire Chevy. Arms spread, the *vatos* threatened Silver, who had mistakenly made eye contact, by yelling, "*¡Y qué? ¡Chinga tu madre y tu puta en su stupid gavacho ranfla!*" The tattoos on their arms and chests were blue as bruises. Their shaved scalps were also blue.

"What did they say?" Laura asked.

"They said you have a nice ride."

Laura appeared confused.

"A nice Volvo."

Laura smiled into the rearview mirror, wiggled her manicured fingernails at them, and next brought her happy smile onto two old men—*borrachos*—with quarts of piss-colored beer at their feet, heavy as sledge hammers from years of work. One scratched at the gray sprouts in his underarm and waved that hand at Laura.

"A rich tradition of simple living," Laura cried. "I wish I could join them and listen to their stories of old Mexico."

She wants to do this Chicana thing, Silver thought, and thought, I'm going to ask her about her daughter, Jenny. But when he opened his mouth to inquire, his right hand came up and closed it. Amazed by the sudden impulse of his hand, he turned it over, mystified. His body parts, he perceived, functioned separately from what he really wanted to do. Silver began to theorize that perhaps the body made decisions separate from the central command called the brain, or why else did so many men get into fights they were certain to lose? His mouth, however, did open to ask how Wesley could allow her to come to East LA.

"We have a sister church," she answered. "The Mighty Rock Baptist Church."

It was Silver's turn to be confused. "A sister church?"

She frowned at Silver as she ignored his inquiry. "Poor baby, I'm sorry for calling you a bastard." She had conferred that title on him, as well other honorary distinctions, for what she had rightly understood as his attempt to leave town without a last smooch and a huggy good-bye. She was sorry because she didn't know that his father had abandoned him when he was but an embryo without the yet defined shapes of skinny arms, crooked legs, a potato nose, or a head full of problems—the sum of his person forty-one years later. She told him that her own father died several years ago, and it pained her immensely. She explained her tragedy while unwrapping a foil of Juicy Fruit chewing gum and gently fingering the gunk of mascara from the corner of her right eye. "Do you forgive me?" She batted her eyelashes and pouted.

Silver had no recourse except to say, "Of course."

She fanned her eyelashes with a greater vigor. "Do you really, my hot tamale?" She stared down at his crotch as her arm, like a crane on a construction site, moved from the steering wheel and rested the claw of her hand on his thigh.

"Yeah, really." His attention was immediately drawn away from his thigh. "Hey, pull over."

They were passing East Los Angeles City College (ELAC) and Silver, the all-time escape artist from bad lovers, was presented an opportunity to ditch Laura. His good buddy, Salvador What's-His-Name, taught Chicano psychology there, his lectures babbling with unproven remarks about race, such as why whites genetically preferred milk (a source of their 'white power' racism) over all beverages, not counting redneck bikers from Bakersfield who had a liking for beer in kegs. He also had a thing for women, as long as they weren't too ugly, and had been married three times, possibly more, with kids born of his quickie lovemaking in all the western states except Oregon, though his old amigo wasn't sure of that because he had received crank calls from that state on Father's Day. It had been seven years since they had seen each other, and then, as Silver recalled, both were sleeping in his car because Salvador's wife, Olga, a house painter by day, an artist by night, had locked them out the house. Silver had been there to do a poetry reading on campus.

Laura steered the Volvo to the curb, parked it in a yellow zone, and brought out a placard that said "Clergy." She posted it on the dashboard.

Silver was about to ask if the use of the placard, usually employed during funerals, was against religious rules. But he instructed his tongue to lie back down when it started to point out her hypocrisy. After all, they weren't going to a funeral, or were they?

But Silver did ask, with some anxiety, "Laura, have you ever seen a guy in a black suit running around campus?" He was beginning to think that perhaps seeing that figure—plus getting those absurd phone calls—was the result of things falling on his head. Maybe he was making it all up, hallucinating.

Laura narrowed her eyes at him. "What are you talking about, buddy boy?"

Silver continued, "A guy. He's not very tall. He wears a black suit and has a funny little hat."

"Baptists don't wear black suits. Jewish people wear black suits. The Mafia people. Funeral directors. But not us."

Silver dropped the subject and, in order to keep her mood perky, led her promptly onto the campus of ELAC.

It was lunchtime and a back-to-college fair was in full swing. Students were milling on the lawn and under the canopied arbor with vines that were nearly leafless from the change of summer to autumn. Tables were situated there and under trees. Balloons banged heads in a light wind and a radio provided entertainment.

Laura walked hastily in front of Silver and the lawn-sniffing Baloney.

Silver was struck by how the once political environs had changed. Most of the students appeared Hispanic, not Chicano, meaning they were dressed fashionably in athletic shoes, not huaraches. He observed that a cross section of the populace—students, faculty, and what he assumed were counselors in neckties—had discovered burgers and fries. As a result, they were all robust in figure. Silver discerned his shadow, thin as a Popsicle stick on a sidewalk, and momentarily felt sorry for himself; he was seemingly the only one not eating three or four times a day. But his sorrow quickly vanished when he witnessed a young, heavy-set woman who required both hands to get up from behind a card table that was furnishing information about the Republican Party. He also observed card tables that promoted a Latina sorority, a Hispanic water polo team, and international student exchange programs to France, Austria, and Holland. What about Mexico? El Salvador, Nicaragua, or Guatemala?

Where did the true Chicanos go? Silver pondered, his right hand stroking his beard. It seemed like only yesterday when young men had long hair instead of combed locks, and wild plans of revolt.

Silver meandered among the tables, picking up free literature and putting it back down. He became mute when, within ten feet, he came upon his long-lost friend, Salvador What's-His-Name, seated at a card table bearing "Jesus Is Your Amigo" brochures. True, Salvador's hair had grayed in places and his jowls hung like pears. But it struck Silver as a miracle to find him. Silver was particularly curious how his friend's nose had shrunk, possibly from the lack of booze or, perhaps, the magical, potato-peeler-like implement seen in *TV Guide*. His friend had also put on considerable weight, which was noticeable in spite of the tentlike guayabera that flowed almost to his knees. His fingers were pudgy as sausages. And instead of a UFW pin on his lapel, Salvador sported a tiny cross.

"Laura," a backpedaling Silver cried hoarsely. She was leafing through literature about adopting Hispanic children. But before Silver could get Laura's attention, Salvador rose

from his chair—both hands on the table top for leverage—
and beckoned, "Silvestre Mendez, come here!"

To Silver, the sound of his name resonated with a bibli-
cal calling, like Moses throwing down his staff and creating
a snake. He had to wonder if his friend was a Jehovah's
Witness, the sect whose sole purpose was to ring doorbells
and bother homeowners seated comfortably in front of their
TVs. At least the Salvation Army helped the sick and put
clothes on people. And Baptists? They at least liked sex.

Salvador came around the card table, with the greeting:
"Silvestre! You old, Chicano dawg!"

"Salvador!" Silver bellowed in return, but praying with
all his heart that his name was just that, a name, instead of
a calling to save lost souls. Silver liked himself pretty much
in his current form, though he could use a little more meat
around the middle for the coming winter.

The two hugged in an *abrazo* that all but realigned Silver's
vertebrae and may have added an inch to his height, thus
thinning him out even more. Salvador was prompted to
comment, once they disengaged, "*Chihuahua,* you look like
some hungry wolf come down from the mountains."

Silver would have rocked on his heels, but his huaraches
had none. Hurt by his friend's description, he nearly issued a
spiteful comment about the gain of flab under his friend's
chin, but he parried that instinct. Why begin their reunion
with a confrontation? "What's going down?"

Salvador smiled. "Jesus."

Silver smiled behind his beard, his pinkish tongue showing briefly before retracting back into its hermit's cave. Is
this the *vato* who, after parties broke up in the wee hours of
morning, drank from half-empty beer cans full of cigarette

butts? Is this the *vato* who passed his hands over the rear
ends of women who were not his wives, who reneged on
promises to repay loans, who came to parties empty-handed
but ate and drank like there was no tomorrow, and who
taught gibberish in his courses but branded the administration racists when he was not promoted? Silver smiled and
remarked, "Cool."

Salvador giggled, rattling the change and keys in his pockets. "Yes, Jesus is cool."

"What are you, a Jehovah's Witness?"

"Baptist," Salvador answered.

The word Baptist appeared to be a cue for Laura, as she
returned from a table clutching a flyer about the clean-
water initiative in *el barrio*. She sidled up to Silver. "This is
great! We don't have anything like this at our college!"

Salvador dragged his attention to Laura's face and then,
slowly, as his eyelids grew heavy, swung downward to appraise
her breasts, both separate in their monstrous bra but
companions when it came to lovemaking. His pupils dilated
as they settled on her white blouse.

Silver picked up this transgression and pulled on his beard
for a piece of wisdom on how he could put Salvador's weakness
to use. A single, rusty gear of connivance creaked in his mind.
This is too easy, he thought, but it must be done! "Salvador,
this is my friend, Laura Skaggs, and she wants to get to know
. . . *la comunidad.*"

"*Mucho gusto en conocerla,*" Salvador greeted, hand
extended, his vanity apparent to all as he inhaled greatly to
suck in his gut. By this action, his guayabera hung shorter
for a few seconds, then lengthened when he couldn't hold
his breath any longer. His gut, like magic, reappeared and

cast a tremendous shadow at his feet.

Laura accepted Salvador's hand and pounded the heel of her shoe in excitement. "God, I love '*mucho*.'"

Salvador bristled his eyebrows, baffled. Then he arranged a smile on his face and said, "I would be happy to show you around. *Hay mucho que ver en* East *Los*."

Laura cried, "There it is again—'*mucho!*'" Then, sucking in her own pronounced gut, thus augmenting the breasts that made Salvador's pupils dilate even further, she twanged, "*Gracias.*"

Silver turned away from the mating scene and viewed the sky. He could foresee a future that included neither Laura nor Salvador. He saw himself back in Oakland, he and Tyronne watching a Raiders game on a Sunday afternoon. Both of them would be slouching on the couch, gobbling pork rinds and washing them down with quarts of beer. For this to actually occur, he needed funds. He patted his back pocket: his check was still there, along with the two twenties in his sock.

When he returned his attention to Laura and Salvador, Silver noted that they were scandalously close—a pucker from either would have closed the distance between the two and had them actually smooching. Was this love at first sight? Would Salvador be lured by Laura's horniness that eventually rubbed a man the wrong way? Would he put aside his newfound faith and return to the nasty habit of butt-pinching? Something was occurring between the two, as their eyes were plainly glassy. Silver fought the urge to tiptoe away, thus leaving the two to their own devices. The spell was broken when Baloney barked.

Salvador tilted his head down. "Is that your *perrito?*"

"Yeah, he's my hound dog," Silver gushed with pride.

Baloney wagged his tail and exhibited his tongue.

Laura, seeing that the canine was a large issue in the hearts of men, played up her charms: "I just love doggies. And this one's such a cutie!" She snapped her fingers at Baloney, who rolled his tongue back into his mouth. She threw a kiss at Baloney and winked boldly at Silver. She then turned on the spikes of her high heels and faced Salvador. "And I can't forget this fella! You're an ol' doggie, too." She blew a kiss at Salvador, who played it up and caught it on his cheek.

Silver stepped back involuntarily, convinced more than ever that the body could act on its own, especially in moments of danger. He sensed danger now. He took a step backward and blurted out, "Laura, she's Baptist."

Laura, hands coming to her hips, frowned. Clouds of anger passed over her pupils.

"I mean—" Silver didn't know what he meant.

Laura cooled immediately. She played with an earring and, with pride, confessed, "My husband is President of Simi Valley Baptist College."

Salvador, mouth open, patted his cheek in disbelieve. "You don't say!"

"You know the college?" Laura asked.

"Why, yes. Every true Baptist knows its excellent tradition."

Silver rolled his eyes again. He could see that Salvador was working on Laura. Then he understood how Laura, the bud of her tongue flittering in and out, was working on Salvador. They deserved each other, these two Baptists, and Silver deserved to get away.

"Hey, you know," Silver began, "I'm going to go and check out La Casa de Bellas Artes."

La Casa de Bellas Artes was a Chicano studio and art gallery, a showcase of the best—and worst—artwork of the times. Silver had frequented the place back in the late 1970s. He had partied with the artist crowd and read his poetry there, usually to an audience of other poets too drunk or loaded to sit in chairs, so they propped themselves against the walls, examining their fingers. True, it had been a wild time. And also true, it was a looser time when the Chicanitos wanted to bake their own cake and to eat it too— a revolution for the people and a bomb of a party during which beer bottles were tilted like trumpets into thirsty mouths. It would be good to go back and see what happened to his audience. Maybe they were still sitting against the walls with their brains ruined.

"*Oye,*" Salvador said, putting his hand on Silver's shoulder. "We got this youth conference tomorrow. Why don't you come by and read your stuff?"

Pensively, Silver pulled on his beard.

"I can work it out for you to get three hundred *bolas.*"

The money sounded good, but the promise empty.

"But I don't have any of my poems."

"I have one of your books somewhere." He pointed vaguely at where his office was situated.

Silver licked his lips. "*Pues,* do I need to fill out forms to get paid?" he inquired directly.

Salvador laughed. "*Mira este chavalo.* Always concerned about *la feria.*"

Silver's stomach growled.

Salvador laughed harder. "You skinny so-and-so. You were always the hungry one."

"You got that right, Homes." Silver then pulled Salvador

aside, while Laura clicked her fingers at Baloney, who had rolled on his back and was sunning his pinkish belly. "Hey, dude, are you *really* religious?"

Salvador took Silver by the arms. His face became stern. "Peer into my eyes."

Silver, inches away from Salvador, gazed into his eyes and made out first his own reflection—his beard was a tangled mess, his nose the shape of an Idaho potato—and then, after much concentration, the image of a woman with curves appeared and passed lovingly over Salvador's wet lenses. *Chihuahua!* Silver thought. The scam! He worked out of Salvador's grip and turned. Indeed, a young woman was passing, her beauty so evident that it would bring tears to the eyes of a born-again Christian.

The three went off to a Mexican lunch, Salvador's treat, and Salvador repeated the word *"mucho"* to get Laura laughing and singing "Oh, such a rich culture—pass me the tortilla chips." Salvador told two clean jokes about Catholics and Laura's bejeweled hand rose and fell on his forearm as she flirted over her combination plate number two. She praised him as the *número uno* crack-up.

Finally, as lunch wound down and napkins wiped greasy fingers, Salvador leaned into Silver's shoulder and whispered in spicy Spanish for Silver to get lost.

The juice of chicken tacos was on Laura's lips, and after she tidied with lip-gloss, she issued a similar verdict to Silver, though in English: "See you later, my former hot tamale. *Mucho! Mucho!*"

Silver couldn't walk fast enough out of that restaurant.

★

Poets end up flat on their backs in graveyards, and Silver

was equipped emotionally to look ahead to his own eventual demise when his casket—a pine job with cheaply forged handles, and a couple of army blankets, not a velvety lining, on which to rest—would be lowered into the earth. He walked among the headstones of the well-maintained Chinese cemetery on Eastern Avenue, seeking the stone that marked a good friend of his, Larson Wong, poet, street astrologer, and owner of one of the biggest bongs in East LA. Larson had fallen to his death from a two-tiered deck, at a time when he was at the height of his career and, everyone assumed, high on Bolinas's best grass. Silver had attended that Terrace City party, but he was passed out on a couch, Larson's bong resting on his chest and smoke uncurling from his nostrils when he began to snore. When he awoke three hours later, the partygoers were gone, replaced by the police and paramedics.

Silver remembered how he could barely stand at the funeral, so full of grief was he, grief because a dear friend was gone and his parents cried in Mandarin, in English, and in Spanish. For them, the world had come to an end. How their tears watered the very lawn at their tiny feet. Silver, too, seeded the lawn with his own watery sorrow, but only managed in yellowing the blades of grass. His system was toxic from so many drugs, which he mostly refrained from after Larson's death.

Silver strolled among the headstones, some of which were off kilter, others straight as accountants and may, in fact, have been the property of those dead professionals, their longer fingers still fidgeting from working numbers. The rows and rows of headstones reminded him of a drive-in movie theater: the casket pulled in, parked, and a headstone was thrown up to watch the greatest movie, the shifting fortunes of stars in the night sky.

"Where are you, brother?" Silver lamented.

Wind parted the leaves of the trees, but offered no answer.

"I'm sorry you fell off like you did."

A black bird rustled in a chinaberry tree.

"I heard your mother died."

A sprinkler along the brick wall spurted on and began to drench the ivy.

Silver got comfy under a tree and watched a gardener watch him. But when the gardener, who had been gathering wilted flowers from the graves, left, Silver began writing a poem called "Little Man in the Black Suit."

Black stars live in the end of your gun.
The moon is in your eye, little sucker,
And from the floor where I lay I spit in it.
You have your coke, you have your big laugh
From your small mouth. You strike me
And I fall. Big deal, little sucker.
I'm going to rise like an Aztec bird
And jump into the branches of an apple tree.

As Silver composed in a small, spiral-bound notepad—his Chicano palm pilot, he jokingly told Salvador—Silver reflected on the notion that each city in California had a pariah who wore a black suit and came bearing drugs, or death itself. Thus, the black suit of a funeral director. Thus, the gun that won every argument over flesh and bone. He wrote this truth in his poem, and wrote a second one about memory, or the loss of memory, mainly his, though he did make references to Mrs. Bartlett's husband, dead of

Alzheimer's. He licked his pencil, wrote of footsteps erased by wind and the shuffle of people trying to get somewhere. He had to admit that he tried to get somewhere. After all, he did take the job at Simi Valley Baptist College. Didn't that have the whiff of ambition? Moreover, didn't he write three books of poems and garner a small readership back in the 1970s when his name meant something? Fame doesn't come back, he reasoned and then pouted that everyone but himself was eating regularly.

For the first time in years, Silver experienced the power of words, and he roared his message in his notepad, but had nothing to say when a *vato* came up from behind and whacked him on his forehead with a garden trowel. He whacked him two more times, before Silver sensed something was terribly wrong.

Silver fell over like a potted plant. He groaned and kicked his legs up to his chest, his eye that was closest to the grass viewing two ants carrying a log—no, the leg of a praying mantis—in their jaws. After a long minute, he righted himself and through the blood that was washing over his lips, he groggily asked his assailant, "Why did you do that?"

The *vato*, with a shaved head that might have belonged to one of the three he had seen earlier, rubbed his index finger and thumb together, the international sign for money. When the *vato* raised the trowel again, Silver obeyed the gravity of fear, toppled over on his own recourse, and let the *vato* frisk his pockets. He played dead among the truly dead, who only spoke in whispers when the Santa Ana winds sliced through the headstones.

Chapter Twelve

During the heist at the cemetery, the *vato* discarded the gardening trowel, threw two punches at Silver's bean bag head, and then threw a fit when Silver's wallet produced no more than a few useless articles. What in the world was he going to do with a receipt from the Rescue Mission in Richmond? Or a BART ticket? The young man yanked off Silver's huaraches and discovered the paycheck he had moved from his back pocket and hidden with the two twenties in his left sock.

"*¡Fuchi!* You stink!" the *vato* yelled, staggering backward, fingers pinching his nostrils at the odor of Silver's tired hooves. But his dull eyes brightened as he read the amount on the Simi Valley Baptist College check: $2,737.11.

"You a teacher, *¿ese?*"

With his mouth filling with blood, Silver nodded his head. He sat up and pleaded for mercy by smearing blood on his pants. He shooed Baloney, who was peering from around a weatherworn headstone. Why get his dog involved?

"OK, then fuck you! I hate *puto* teachers!" He shouldered Silver's plastic garbage bag that contained his clothes.

There were plenty of people to witness the robbery, but they were all dead. Baloney couldn't speak up either. The gardener, who had been picking wilted flowers, was down on his knees, in prayer it seemed, fixing a broken sprinkler head at the far end of the cemetery that was being made shipshape for new arrivals. Silver rose up to a sitting position, not unlike Lazarus, and wiggled his pale toes.

"*Cabrón,*" he whimpered after the *vato* hurdled two low-lying headstones and kicked a can of fresh flowers from another grave. He deplored his wretched luck that had followed him from Simi Valley to East *Los,* and would probably follow him back to Oakland and Hayward. He eased himself down, arms at his side, and mused: "Is this what the dead would see if they could?" The sky was yellow with smog and absent of both fair and unfair gods. Two devil gnats were circling his nose.

With Baloney in tow, Silver walked meekly into La Casa de Bellas Artes, holding not his much-scathed head but the pair of new socks that Laura had bought him. He had used them to soak up blood that ran pale instead of dark, a sign to Silver, a health nut from unregimented fasting, that he had better start eating more meat. He was greeted by a guy he had met years ago, a guy he might have partied with. What was his name again?

"Hey, man!" the guy yelled from across the gallery. He approached Silver in wide strides, as if a horse was between his legs. "The last time I saw you, you was bleeding, *ese.* What, that was like ten years ago and you're still all fucked up?" His giggling revealed front teeth trimmed in gold, and a weird humor. He led Silver like an old man to a folding chair, comforting him with, "Don't worry, *viejo,* at least you're alive."

He left and came back with paper towels and a can of Pepsi. He threw a Slim Jim to Baloney, who carried it to a corner of the gallery.

"Seeing blood on you like this, I feel like hitting somebody." He punished his left outstretched palm with a belt from his right fist.

Silver recalled the name of his patron saint of bloodied faces: Ramon. "Don't let it be me, Ramon."

Ramon pushed Silver's head to one side. "Who whipped you?"

"I don't know."

Ramon played with the large mole on his chin. "*Pues,* man, it's hard to go and kick ass if you don't know." Ramon winced at the gash on Silver's forehead. "You know, *ese,* when I was in the Marines they taught us if we got a gut wound where like your *tripas* are falling out, you could use shoelaces to close it up." Ramon clicked his tongue at Silver's huaraches. "Oh, man, I'm sorry but you ain't got no shoelaces!" He slapped his thighs, laughing, and then hardened as the coals of anger lit up his pupils. "I'm looking for this asshole who owes me money. You artists never pay your loans. Shit, man, I did some pin striping for the *pinche cabrón,* and he says he was going to do this and that for me. I'm going to do some of this." He popped his left fist into his right palm.

Silver closed his eyes and saw stars.

Ramon stopped nursing Silver, stepped away, hiking up his pants, and scowled at the artwork on the walls. "No wonder you assholes are poor. You guys can't paint straight."

On the walls hung artwork that was abstract and whacked out.

"I ain't a painter."

"I thought you was." He carried his attention to Silver's feet. "You got no shoes, *¿qué no?* I thought all you artist dudes are poor and shit."

"I'm a poet."

"There you go, Homes. I was almost right." Ramon wagged his head at a poorly executed oil painting of an old man watering his lawn. "These fuckers couldn't paint their fingernails. Their hands don't work too good, so how do they wipe their asses? You know what I mean?"

Silver reserved the right to be silent, though he glanced at the painting. Ramon was right. The old man appeared to be holding a stick, and the dog at his feet resembled a suitcase.

Ramon jerked his head at Silver. "Hey, Homes, you know Palo?"

Silver sort of remembered his name. "A skinny dude?"

"Nah, man, a fat dude. A rhino. You're the skinny dude!"

Silver shook his head.

"You see him, you tell him that Ramon's going to kick his ass." Ramon chewed his lower lip, hungry to throw blows. He clicked his fingers at Silver. "Yeah, man, I remember you from way back, and I think you had just got beat up in the parking lot by one of your poet homies."

Silver remembered all too clearly. He had mouthed off to a sober poet with four books and a lot more muscle.

"You were bleeding like you are right now."

Silver grew sullen. He wished a flying saucer would crash through the ceiling and take Ramon away—for good, for everyone's good.

"If you see that *gordo* Palo, tell it like it is, see! *¿Entiendes Mendez?*"

Silver was grateful that he didn't owe Ramon a dime because he wouldn't be able to pay. Ramon was a body-and-fender man, and Silver had seen him lift an engine block from the floor to a workbench like it was his lunch box. It may have been his lunch because Ramon was all iron. Shirt off, he would display chest muscles large as hubcaps.

Ramon bid farewell with a clap on Silver's shoulders, but hesitated in the doorway. He looked left, then right, and decided to go right with both fists closed.

Silver chugged his Pepsi and wiped his face clean of blood

and nervous sweat. It was hard being in the same room with a lot of bad student art and a body-and-fender man with a grudge. The combination made him jittery.

He washed in the men's room and would have studied his dirty face in the dirty mirror except he didn't want to scare himself. The day itself was taking care of that. When he came out of the restroom, wiping his hands on his pants because there were no paper towels in the dispenser, he ran into Palo, the fat dude.

The two studied each other, as if the other was a piece of artwork. A fly came between them for a moment and then vanished.

"Just run," Silver warned, the best advice he was going to give all day. "Go left, man."

Palo didn't need an explanation or a road map. At once, he was out the door, the fastest fat man in East *Los* of all time.

"You need some help?"

Silver was startled at the sound of a soft greeting.

"The gallery isn't open."

Silver spun around, confused, and then made out a figure on the staircase that led to the upstairs offices. He was facing a woman in her late thirties. He knew the face, though not intimately because, let's face it, it was just too lovely. Silver was reminded of fruits, a strawberry and a cherry. He was tripping on a poetic mood and was tempted to whip out the notepad from his back pocket. He lowered his face, embarrassed by the tragedy of his recent beating. The pulsating wound was closed with the beginning stitches of a natural scab, and he feared, ridiculously he admitted, that it might reopen from his rising blood pressure. Her beauty was natural, unlike the three walls of skilled and unskilled art around them.

When he gazed up, the poetry began again: her eyes were

almond-shaped, like Laura's, but with a light that shone without bitterness. What was her long hair but a lash for a man's back, an exquisite punishment?

Transfixed by her presence, he opened his trap and uttered the first thing that came into his mind: "Nah, I was just kicking in the neighborhood and I wanted to check out what's going down." He should have stuck one of the bloody socks, now on the folding chair, into his mouth. What kind of speech was that! Nothing befitting his rank of veteran poet.

The woman descended the stairs, and Silver tried not to stare openly at the push of her hips, the right one going up as the left went down. He tried to keep his pleasure contained because he didn't wish to smile like a vampire with bloody teeth. He rolled his tongue over his teeth and prayed that the Pepsi had freshened his breath. Or at least drained the blood from the fissures between his front fangs.

"Hello, Silver," she greeted.

She knows me?

"You don't remember me, do you?"

Silver intended to make time once he got back to Oakland to consult a doctor. The doctor could shove his head in one of those machines—a cat scanner, or whatever they called it—to judge whether he had a tumor or simply pockets of air in his brain.

Silver admitted that he could not place her face. Their relationship was as mysterious as the artwork on the walls.

"I was Larson's girlfriend."

Silver's left knee buckled. How could he forget! He bowed his head, and his thoughts turned to the Chinese cemetery. The grounds were peaceful, with wind slicing through the trees and headstones and producing a sound that was the language of the dead. A sprinkler was spraying the dusty ivy,

and a single bird—Larson's reincarnated double?—was singing its two-note repertoire on the pagodalike rooftop of the
building where the mowers were stored.

"Elena?" Silver guessed after he raised his head.

"That's right—Elena."

Elena caught sight of Silver's wound. "What happened?" She
peered beyond Silver at the bloody sock in the chair and then
caught sight of Baloney, who had the Slim Jim between his front
paws and was gnawing the meaty lollipop with pleasure.

She departed without a word, and Silver figured that, like
everything good in his life, she too left without so much as a
good-bye. In fact, there was no good-bye, unless it was in the
wince that fanned out a set of wrinkles at the corners of her eyes.

But she returned quickly with car keys jingling in her hands.

She drove him—and Baloney whining for another Slim
Jim—to her house in Temple City, nine miles from East *Los*.
With Q-tips and cotton balls, she washed the wound and
told him to hush when the alcohol burned like fire. She let
him lie down on the couch, where he drowsed with a magazine, slept, and woke at dusk. A single star showed through
the high window in the living room. No, as he sat up groggily, he saw that it was a streetlight.

"Where's Baloney?"

Elena tilted her head, bewildered.

"The dog."

Baloney walked in unannounced. Silver was momentarily
jealous that his dog drifted over to Elena instead of to his
invalid master. She lowered her slim arm and scratched his
neck until he closed his eyes from the pleasure.

Silver's jealousy deepened. God, if only I were that dog,
he thought.

"Why the name . . . 'Baloney'?" Elena asked with a smile.

"Don't ask," Silver responded, also with a smile.

"What can I ask then?" She pulled her hand from Baloney's fur and placed it on her lap.

Silver munched his lower lip. He breathed in and exhaled. He told her that she didn't have to ask anything, that he would gladly spill the beans, the sum of his past seven years since Larson's death. He told her how he worked as a teacher's aide, as a library aide in the children's section, and as an aide in a nursing home for the aged—jobs he took and abandoned or that abandoned him whenever state monies ran out. He said that he still wrote poetry, but not much, and that his mother had given up on him. He described his trip to Spain and—he gulped—his sentence at a road camp in Avenal, where he re-paved country roads no one wanted to go down. In road camp, he painted rocks, too, and broke branches over his knees as they cleaned up canals where fish gasped on the oily surface and used condoms floated by. The crime for his three-month sentence: drunk driving in a stolen golf cart.

With the last confession, Elena pressed her hands over her ears, laughed, and chided Silver for being a bad boy.

Silver had to agree.

"What are you doing around here?" Elena asked. She had moved her hand back onto Baloney's neck.

Silver munched for another taste of his lower lip. He sighed and asked, "You know anything about Baptists?"

Elena shook her head.

"Do you know a place called Blanche?"

Elena shook her head again.

Silver touched one of his older wounds. "I've been teaching at a college in Simi Valley."

"In Simi Valley?" She shifted uncomfortably in her chair. "Don't Republicans live there?"

Silver nodded.

"I don't want to know any more."

Silver agreed that it was better that she remained innocent of his ludicrous migration from one problem to the next. God, to narrate what had occurred in the last four days. And to bring up Laura! He pictured poor Salvador on his back trying to climb out of that position as her powerful rump rose and fell. He then had a change of heart. Serves him right!

Silver walked across the living room and sat in the chair next to Elena.

"And how are you?"

"Single."

"Happy, then?"

"Happier than if I were married."

Silver gazed around a living room aglow with loudly political Chicano artwork on walls and tables, some, no doubt, gifts and others purchased cheaply, for artists had always hung around Larson and, he supposed, Elena. A portrait of Frida Kahlo, inventor of the one-eyebrow look now in vogue, was the centerpiece of tin stars on the wall. A red Chinese umbrella screened the light on the ceiling, and a curtain of multicolored beads separated the living room from the dining room. A Mexican *bolero* sobbed from a radio in the kitchen. There was the scent of incense in the air and the scent of candles. What prayers she said in front of them, he could only guess.

"Do you work at La Casa?"

She pulled her hair behind her ear, as if she wanted to hear the question again. But she understood. "No, I work at an insurance company. Crooks." She directed her attention to Baloney, lifted his floppy ear, and whispered: "Crooks." She then straightened up in her chair and provided Silver with her history as a volunteer bookkeeper at La Casa.

Silver could see that she was sad. She's got her act together, but she's sad. Her entire room, her flowing hippie dress, the music on the radio, and the VW bug were relics of the '70s. They were relics, though she was lovely and timeless.

"Elena," he said softly. "I'm sorry about Larson."

Elena played with the hem of her skirt. "We were going to get married. He was such a fool. You were a fool, too."

Silver could only offer youthfulness as an excuse for their foolishness. Yes, that would have explained their behavior. But he only turned his hands up on his lap and stared at the dirty lines of misfortune "Yeah, we were stupid." And for Silver, the present times were no better. What unemployed man gets robbed in a cemetery? Who gladly hands off his lover to a born-again Christian? What Chicano lets himself be caught on videos carrying a portrait of Reagan through a parking lot?

"When did you first meet Larson?"

Silver pulled on his beard. When was it? He could not bear to face Elena and instead flipped his hands on his lap like pancakes and inspected the leathery skin burned by the sun and the occasional odd job. Silver had to admit to himself that he hadn't known Larson well. They hung together and got loaded and laughed from the back seats of speeding cars. He remembered stealing pickles at a supermarket and eating them in the cemetery where Larson would be buried. They had been young men using up their time foolishly.

"Oh, Larson," she called faintly neither to Silver nor Baloney, who, with his shaggy head propped on his paws, had one eye open to their talk.

Silver bowed his head and shaded his eyes, embarrassed that he couldn't remember when he and Larson first met. Was his memory gone? A pail with a hole and the water flowing out? He heard Elena's footsteps, the opening of the refrigerator, and something cool being poured into glasses. She returned bearing two blue glasses.

"Thank you," he said as he carefully took the glass. He could use a beer, preferably a Japanese import, but didn't complain when he raised the drink to his mouth and sipped. Tea. Sun tea, a concoction of the 1970s. If only she would offer him unsalted sunflowers, or a pinch of Granola, fiber that scrubbed the insides clean—hippie grub from a decade that might come back.

Silver showered a full half-hour, and when he got out, pink from the first true scrubbing in two days, not counting the drenches at the college gym, he discovered on her bed a fresh shirt and a pair of pants ready to be filled. They were Larson's clothes, faded and out of style, folded neatly for god knows how long in a scented drawer. Silver sniffed and made out the scent of lavender, the scent that flavored Elena's skin. He put them on and used the comb and toothbrush placed on the paisley bedspread.

He wiped the bathroom mirror fogged with steam. Is this me? he asked of the watery features on the glass. In the dark, he pulled on the string that worked the overhead light and, with a cautious tenderness, combed his stringy locks.

He set his old clothes balled up in a corner.

When he returned to the living room neither said anything. Elena was already holding her car keys in her lap. He sipped from his tea and said, "Let's go."

She drove him back to La Casa.

"Be happy," Elena whispered into his neck, and kissed that neck and remarked how sweet he smelled.

"I smell like you."

Elena appeared baffled. Then she blossomed into a smile. "My shampoo."

When he got out of the car, he wagged his finger at Baloney. "Stay!"

"Silver!" she yelled, eyes wide, startled.

"You'll like him. You'll have to."

"No, Silver, he's yours! You need him!" He closed the door, and Baloney quickly moved from the floorboard to the passenger's seat, his head hanging out the window. Silver closed his hand around Baloney's snout and shook it a good-bye.

★

Silver sized up the crowd at La Casa de Bellas Artes and, over the din of chattering mouths buttoned down with chrome balls on tongues, made out the syrupy introduction of the poet who had bloodied his nose seven years ago. The poet was being introduced as one of the best ever—forget Shakespeare! Let Frost wander through the woods forever!—who, with seven books, all classics, linked people to literature, or why would so many of his fans be present for his first work of prose, a novel about a dysfunctional family whose abusive father raised his voice when his children came home with B's on their report cards. The MC twisted the metal knob that resided between his lower lip and his chin, gazed slowly around the gallery space and informed the crowd that the poet, *el mero mero*, was irreplaceable, a genius. After all, didn't he win a MacArthur Fellowship? He had to be a genius.

"My brown *nalgas*," Silver muttered in the doorway. "He · don't know the genius of street pain! Let him eat brie!" Most certainly he was jealous and wounded, but to keep from recreating the scene of his ass-whipping in the parking lot seven years ago, Silver came to his senses. He ought to just leave, walk back to ELAC, hitch a ride back to Simi Valley to collect Jason, his protégé, and get back to Oakland.

Grief overwhelmed Silver when he spied his bloody sock still under the leg of a folding chair. It went unnoticed like he, winner of no awards and author only of books yellowing in cardboard boxes in a dank closet. While the sock's soaked-up blood was dry, Silver clenched his fist and cried in his heart, "I'm alive."

And he also cried through his cupped hands rolled into a megaphone: "Fuck you, fake asshole poet! Brie-eating caca head!"

Heads turned, but Silver was quick in his huaraches and galloped down the street, his long hair slapping his shoulders. No herd of poetry zealots pursued him, confirming in Silver's mind that none of the audience really cared for the celebrated poet. Then, as he slowed his trot, he began to wonder whether they didn't care about *him*, Silver, that his outburst was mistaken as a lunatic rambling from a street person without socks.

He walked along Whittier Boulevard, which was loud with Mexican music blasting from the moist caverns of dirty bars. He breathed in the aroma of a *panadería*, jumped over a river of water from a man hosing down the front of his upholstery shop, and sidestepped three *mocoso* kids on low-rider bikes. He window-shopped at a jeweler's and picked out a watch if he had money. He ground his teeth at the loss of his check and stepped into the shadows of a closed realtor's doorway when he thought he recognized the *vato* who had looted his pockets and socks.

"I want to go home," he chanted five times in a near whisper. He walked block after littered block, weaving between nighttime shoppers and *cholos* with their shirts off but their hairnets on. He divorced himself from the people around him and cut out the smells of overripe fruit in bins outside storefronts.

Silver positioned himself on the edge of a bus stop bench, careful not to smear the bottom of his pants—Larson's pants—with gum, spilled soda, bird droppings, and the film of diesel smoke. He made out the smell of tacos from the roach coach parked across the street. His stomach grumbled, the pipes of his intestines shut down for the last nine hours. *I shouldn't have said no to Elena when she offered to fix me a sandwich,* Silver told himself. He looked into his palms and foresaw the deltas flooded not with ink but with grime and sweat.

If I was going somewhere, I would be there already, he argued philosophically. He worked up this piece of truth and traced the lines of his palms, now darker in the early evening. His beard was wet, his eyes even wetter.

"Jesus," he spoke. He closed his eyes and when he opened them he marveled at the graceful structure. It was the Mighty Rock Baptist Church, the sister church, as Laura had called it. He got up, dusting the bottoms of his pants.

The church was a former synagogue, with a Star of David etched in stone and barely disguised behind a wooden cross. Silver brought out his notepad and wrote a reminder about his bloody sock under the chair and how the trowel the *vato* used on him at the cemetery was a symbol of the shovel that would one day dig his grave. He was writing Elena's name in the book when a hand touched his shoulder. For a moment he believed that a pigeon, national bird of the homeless, had settled on the soup bone of his shoulder.

"Why don't you come in," an elderly gentleman suggested. The man was dressed in a poorly fitting suit gray as a pigeon. "We have bread to make a sandwich."

Silver was aghast that the stranger had assumed that he was homeless. He felt that he should be insulted. Did he really look that disheveled? Still, he followed his benefactor, a shuffler because he was old, perhaps old enough to remember when his church was a synagogue.

Silver was led into the church through the back stairs and down into a basement, where in the harsh fluorescent light he was surprised to find dozens of men and women, all dressed nicely, seated at three long banquet tables. Their Bibles were open. He had expected to find sinners such as himself turning on spits and a turkey-necked pastor basting them with holy water. Admittedly, he was scared, but comforted when the man said, "We have soup if you want."

He was surprised by life's twists and turns, how an hour ago he was shouting at a celebrated poet to fuck off, and the next hour he was being paraded past a Bible study group who would never think of cursing another person. Silver fought the urge to call that phony bard anything but a person, more of a kiss-ass, fake do-gooder, C+ talent.

"What's wrong with me!" Silver asked in a hushed voice.

The man who had been leading him turned and, hand to his ear, asked, "¿Como, hermano?"

Silver just showed him his wet eyes.

The man said, "Oh," turned and prodded Silver into the kitchen. He sat Silver down on a stool.

Silver observed the man—named Moises, he found out—move slowly from the refrigerator to the sink's drain board, where he prepared a sandwich and soup. Silver ate his sandwich with his head bowed and stirred the Campbell's alphabet soup. No matter how he patted the surface of the broth with his spoon, the disorderly letters spelled nothing.

Chapter Thirteen

That night, Silver slept in what he presumed was an abandoned car, rose before daylight, and walked three miles to ELAC, site of the college conference. He arrived early, tired and hungry, and lay on a wooden bench, the bottom of his coffin, he thought morbidly. But he soon scrambled to his feet after he put his hands in his front pockets to fight off the morning chill and fingered a twenty-dollar bill, odorless and crisp, as if it had gone through the wash. "Bless you, Larson!" He praised his angel of mercy and lifted his face skyward, where two small clouds were anchored in the windless morning.

He had breakfast on Larson and remembered the good times over *chorizo con huevos, papas,* and homemade tortillas. He pushed his beard aside as he drank his coffee sweetened with two packets of sugar and looked out the window at a radiator shop, where two German Shepherds paced the contaminated grounds. Too bad he didn't have them when the *vato* jumped him at the cemetery. It would have been a different story.

He returned to the campus, followed signs that read "College Bound," and found Salvador at Student Services.

"*Oye, compa,*" Silver greeted.

Salvador was wearing sunglasses and holding his throat with his hand, as if he were strangling himself. When he pulled the hand away, he revealed dark hickeys.

"Laura?" Silver asked.

Salvador nodded. He nervously undid the top buttons of his fresh guayabera, and displayed more dark hickeys. He was

willing to unbutton all the way to his hairy navel, but Silver
yelled, "I get the picture, *hombre.*" He patted Salvador's paunch.
"Lot of tamales there, bro."

Salvador slapped Silver's hand away. "You sure she's
Baptist?"

"You sure you're Baptist?"

"After last night, *¿quién sabe?*" Salvador pulled his shades
off his nose. His eyes were red from the lack of sleep.

Silver was familiar with the condition. He wished to playfully interrogate Salvador about another part of him that
might be red, but didn't. Instead, he brought up the issue of
getting paid for his poetry reading.

"Tell you the truth, we ain't got no money to pay you.
The pay will be in the kindness you give."

Silver growled over Salvador's false pledge. He bargained,
"OK, then a little *feria* out of your own pocket."

Salvador brought out twenty dollars, mostly ones, from
his wallet.

"So how's Laura?" Silver prayed Laura had her claws in him.

The answer appeared in Salvador's weak smile that colored
his face pink. But the pink vanished as Laura marched around
the corner, her lacquered hairdo on a new foundation for the
day, her face made over with layers of makeup. She was in a
gray business suit and seemed all business because she
stomped over, the bangles on her wrists clattering like
spoons. She dragged Salvador away after she greeted Silver
with a loud, "Hey, my *former* hot tamale! *Mucho! Mucho!
Mucho!*" She kissed him good-bye with her fingertips.

Silver spoke to a dozen at-risk high school students, and
read the one poem in his notepad: "Little Man in the Black
Suit." He told them about books that he had written, available

in libraries, and advised them to stay in school until he was blue around the gills. Meanwhile, the young women teased their hair and chewed gum, and one guy cleaned the teeth of his comb with a matchbook cover.

"Success is a four-year degree!" shouted Silver.

When one asked what college he had graduated from, Silver 'fessed up that he had only forty-seven units under his belt. They looked at him strangely. Sensing that he was losing them, he showed them his Brown Power belt buckle and asked what it meant to be Chicano in contemporary society?

They shrugged. Someone asked if there was going to be something to eat during the break.

Silver didn't reach the students that morning, but by four that afternoon he would reach Simi Valley. He gave his audience a clenched-fist salute and took a hike off the campus, mumbling at his failure at reaching the students and greatly disappointed that there was nothing to eat or drink during the break. He stood at the on-ramp at Atlantic Boulevard, his thumb out and his beard splayed from the wind of passing vehicles. An hour passed as noontime shadows disappeared into the two sickly trees at the bend of the on-ramp. He toed a milk carton and smudged under his huarache a cigar that broke into flakes. For exercise, he shot-put a brick and other debris into the ivy. He was thinking of Laura and Salvador when a carload of the attendees in his workshop banked onto the on-ramp. They didn't even slow down to ask where he was going or if he needed a ride. His eyes met the eyes of one young woman, and her low regard for him quickly flashed by. Silver swallowed. The shame of his claiming that success was a four-year degree, which he hadn't obtained, came to him full force, now in his present position, one foot on the sidewalk and the other in the littered gutter.

Ten minutes later he was beckoned by an older, shaggy-headed brother with a gray beard in a pickup truck loaded with mattresses. He was dressed in green mechanic's overalls. His hat and the tips of his shoes were green from working on lawns. Silver assumed he had more green in his wallet.

Silver happily climbed aboard and right away was struck by the museum of pictures of Jesus taped throughout the cab. A cross swung from the rearview mirror.

"Thanks," Silver said as he settled in. He searched for a seatbelt but found none.

"Oh, you don't need one of those," the brother said as he put the pickup into third gear. Fenders rattled as the pickup merged recklessly into swift traffic. "If Jesus wants you, he'll bring you up, or take you down. Praise Jesus!" He fondled the cross on the rearview mirror. "No telling when you going to go. Some ol' fool might hit us this very moment. No telling, my friend!"

The truck rocked over a pothole, shifting the load of mattresses.

"You making a delivery?" Silver asked.

"To the dump, I am, sir." His grin revealed a blackness where his front teeth once were. He said they were mattresses from a senior citizens' retirement home. "Can you imagine how many died on those?" He hooked his thumb at his load. "I bet you hundreds succumbed on them." He smiled as he checked the side mirror before he glided the truck to the middle lane. "I like that word, 'succumbed.' Fancy word for not being around no more. Like if my truck overturns 'cause of this load. We be in the state of 'succumbed.'"

"Jesus," Silver bleated lowly through his window.

"I know the truth 'cause I'm a sinner! Know that people

made legal love on those mattresses and others fornicated on them like dogs." He paused, regarded the outside mirror, and laughed. "Before they succumbed."

Silver gripped the seat.

"And lots of tears in those mattresses. Pain where they slept. What you expect living in a old people's home? Got to cry there if any place at all." The old brother studied Silver; he pulled on his own gray beard and tapped a work-strong hand on the steering wheel. "Seems like you been hurt by people."

Silver refrained from scratching his itchy scalp, fearing that such action would part his hair and expose his scabs.

"Looks like you been in a fight, too."

Silver shifted his eyes to the mirror on his side when a mattress scooted off the bed, hit the freeway's surface, and began cartwheeling end over end.

"Sir," Silver started, one hand on the dash as he prepared for a crash.

"Lawrence." He extended a hand to Silver and pulled off a photo of Jesus from the ceiling of his cab. "You carry this, my friend, and you be safe."

Silver grinned nervously and then closed his eyes when he saw another mattress ease off the back and fly into the air like a fat angel. He closed his eyes and for the first time in years, amid portraits of Jesuses of every nationality, he prayed.

Silver got off in Culver City and was immediately belted with the insult from a yuppie in a passing convertible, "Get a job!"

Silver boiled under the sun's anger. He kicked a can and threw his thumb out for an hour. No one took the bait; no one even feigned a look of "Sorry, bud." During his stay on a littered spot at an on-ramp no one wished to claim, Silver mulled over how in the world he got the teaching position at Simi Valley Baptist

College. And how did he start up with Laura? When he got back to Oakland, he was going to seek out a friend, Jeannie the Genie, a hypnotist, who might rewire the circuitry that made people remember things. His concern turned to Jason. He had first reduced him to a crybaby rich boy, but now he understood Jason's rage. His rage was wanting to do something—anything.

He got his next ride from a man in a newish Crown Victoria going to Bakersfield, a direct route that would take him up I-5. The man had a beehive for a nose. The reason became clear when he let slip that he was an alcoholic who had abided the twelve-step program of AA, but was once so down in life, so broke, that he drank free hotel bottles of Scope breath freshener for their alcohol content. Silver was strapped in his seatbelt, but almost flew out the window at this confession.

"One time I drank one of those twenty-four-ouncers of Listerine. In Iowa City. Had the freshest breath, but nearly succumbed in a cow pasture when I fell and hit my head."

There was that word again—"succumbed." Silver brought out his notepad and wrote that fancy word beneath "mattress," subjects for future poems.

Silver thanked the man who left him off at the ramp that led to Blanche. He was determined to keep his promise to Jason. He slammed the door of the Crown Victoria, waved a good-bye, and wheeled around to face Detective Ford's idling white cruiser.

"Been waiting for you," Detective Ford said through the rolled-down window. His dog was in the back seat, tongue out and dripping.

Silver got in the front seat. Detective Ford drove three blocks in silence before he asked, "Where's Mrs. Skaggs?"

"Probably in church."

Detective Ford laughed. He studied his laughter in the

rearview mirror.

"What do you want?" Silver braved, with the dog's snout nudging the back of his head like a gun.

The detective looked down at Silver's waist. "I want you to buckle up."

Silver obeyed.

"And I want you to tell me how to keep our community drug free." He asked this with a straight face, while studying his profile in the rearview mirror.

"Drugs are everywhere. You can't stop them." He was going to mention Wal-Mart, the biggest drug dealer in the country, but he remembered that Detective Ford's wife was a pharmacist.

The detective turned into the 7-Eleven, where Silver had tried to cash his check. He parked, left the engine running, and grilled Silver. "This raghead here said you came and bled over his counter."

Silver could make out the clerk behind the counter.

"I would say he's a liar."

"A liar?"

Silver nodded.

Detective Ford sighed. He again became fascinated with his image in the rearview mirror as he said, "I hear you like little boys on bicycles." The statement hung in the air for both to inhale its meaning.

"Nah, I like women."

Detective Ford chuckled and asked, "Like Mrs. Skaggs? She's got some cans on her."

"Yeah, but she's married," Silver said, fidgeting. He swallowed a lozenge of fear when the German Shepherd licked Silver's ear.

"She's married all right. I'm married, but it doesn't stop me from having thoughts. You have thoughts too?"

The German Shepherd ran its wet snout down the back of Silver's neck.

"You like my dog?"

"Friendly fellow."

Detective Ford laughed when the German Shepherd licked the scab above Silver's ear. "He likes you. You must taste mighty good."

Silver opened up his palms. He couldn't read the lines.

"What did I say a couple of days ago?" The detective placed his hand on Silver's knee.

Silver could smell a Denny's Grand Slam breakfast on the peace officer's breath. He didn't know what to answer.

"I said that I don't like your kind." His eyes were hard on Silver, and Silver began to think that the detective was hard down below. His hand would have crabbed up Silver's thigh except the clerk from the 7-Eleven came out with a Big Gulp.

"Hello, officer," the clerk greeted, presenting the syrupy drink through the window. "Your usual."

After a quick slurp through the straw, Detective Ford hooked a thumb at Silver. "So is this the bum?"

The clerk nodded.

To the rearview mirror, he accused, "He says you were trying to pass off a bad check here."

The clerk nodded.

Detective Ford thanked the clerk and told him that he would not be bothered by Mr. Mendez again. "Isn't that right?"

Silver agreed. Beyond that promise, he promised never to shop at a 7-Eleven again.

"I thank you very much," the clerk said, with a half bow. He patted the roof of the cruiser with a palm, and returned to his monopoly of overpriced junk food.

Detective Ford drove Silver to Simi Valley Baptist College.
"Now what did I say?" the detective asked.
"I'm going to be out of town by sundown."
"And when's sundown in Blanche?"
"Six-thirty-seven today. Six-thirty-five tomorrow."
"And how did I hear about the exact time of sundown?"
"You follow the newspaper, and the newspaper is never wrong."

Silver got out of the cruiser but not before the detective stoked his eyes with fire and warned him that if he didn't follow nature's clock—a smoggy sundown—he was going to regret not heeding his warning. "I get real nasty when it's night. Don't be around." He shoved the cruiser into gear and spoke to the rearview mirror that held his eyes, "Let's go, you beast."

Spooked, Silver wheeled around and clomped through the empty campus to Petersen's office, where he was going to look up Jason's telephone number in the phone book. He unlocked and swung open the door—with the air conditioning off for the weekend, the heat was overwhelming. He brought a chair from the office with the intention of resting while the heat escaped, a mistake, he realized, because Mildred banked around the hedge and into the courtyard.

"Professor!" she yelled, waving a batch of papers at him.
For protection, Silver stepped behind the chair.
Mildred speeded her advance by trotting. She was Millie the horse, as her nostrils flared and her hair banged her shoulders like a mane. She stopped in front of him and caught her breath with a hand on her heart.

"Professor, did you finish the school poem?" she asked.
Silver told her no, that he hadn't written the poem.
Mildred looked about her with great caution. In a whis-

per, she said conspiratorially, "I wrote it for you." She circled around the chair, as if they were playing musical chairs, and shoved the poem in Silver's face. "I have six versions, but this is the best. If you want, you can read the others, too."

That was the last thing he wanted. God, to read all six versions while the sun slowly descended and time ran out for him to get out of town. He heard the campus clock strike five o'clock, and didn't he see shadows suddenly lengthen from the hedges?

"No, I'll just read the best one. I know you're a busy man," she said.

He took a seat in the chair, and Mildred backed away a few steps. Silver was her audience of one, and he recalled nights when no one showed up to his poetry readings, except one single soul on Prozac.

"It's about college pride," Mildred said as a way of introduction.

Silver nodded his encouragement.

Mildred swallowed. She asked Silver to hold the other five versions.

"The poem," she started, "is called 'On Flying Wings, Get a Good Education.'"

Silver's armpits began to leak as he scrutinized one of the poems in his hands. His name was under the title of each poem, suggesting that he was the author of that batch. What would his buds think!

Mildred started:

O, let us not forget the shining angel of kindness,
O, let us not forget the campus of education,
You, who for four years hold books in caress
You, who salute life with a mission.

Mildred paused to smile at Silver, who heaved up a big grin on his face. He had a request to ask of her after this private reading was over.

Go forth, saviors of the really true word,
Go forth, saviors of man's work ethic,
Be like a gazelle in a galloping herd,
Be like a hurt soldier's righteous medic.

Mildred stopped to dab her forehead with a white handkerchief. She fluttered her eyelashes flirtatiously at Silver, who picked up his cue and, propelling himself from the chair, roared energetically, "Right on!"

Mildred finished the poem by stomping out the cadence.

"It's really a Shakespearian sonnet," she explained. "But I also have a haiku version."

Oh, my god, Silver thought. Is there no end to this?

She wrestled the batch of poems from Silver, who argued that he was sure that the first version was just perfect, her performance stellar. But, no, she wanted a second opinion and peeled the batch from Silver's grip. She read the haiku:

Books in hand. Mission.
Four years. Mission
Go forth. Medics on Mission.

Mildred paused before she bowed dramatically with a hand on her heart.

Silver clapped, rising from his chair. "Say, Mildred, I was wondering if you have Jason's telephone number."

She appeared confused. "Why?"

Silver had already prepared the answer in his head. "You know the conference I talked about? He's on the committee, and I've got to give him a call."

Mildred ignored Silver.

"Let me read you the ballad version."

Silver clammed up and reminded himself to practice patience. He heard one version that had a tinge of Roy Rodgers, then the Robert Frost version, and then the rap version that made Silver wince as Mildred threw spastic gang signs.

The campus clock struck five-thirty during her reading.

At five-forty, Silver hollered, "Mildred! That's enough!"

Mildred became a startled child. She blinked, brought a hand over her mouth, and began to sob.

Silver was beyond reason. "Listen, I need Jason's number. I'm going to die if I don't get it!"

Mildred sobbed harder and controlled herself long enough to whimper, "You just think about yourself." Then she returned to a shoulder-jerking sob.

Silver made out the sound of the fax machine. Tyronne, he guessed. He ran into the office and, indeed, the machine was unraveling a declaration from his friend. He was declaring war if Silver didn't send his past rent money *pronto*. He finished with a question: "Mexican guy from San Jose won 41 million in the California Lottery and I gotta axe how come you Mexicans always winning? When's the black man's turn? Shit. And how come you ain't the Mexican who ever wins?" He tore the fax out of the machine, cursed his luck, and went outside grumbling.

Mildred was gone.

"*¡Ay, Dios!*" Silver cried, but no god appeared from the smoggy heavens. Instead, Silver spied the little man in the black suit approaching, one hand in his pocket, from the direction of the library. Silver scurried away between buildings and broke into a run once he was off campus. He felt a fire in his lungs, the weight of exhaustion filling the hollows of his legs. All that hustle through the streets—four blocks, then a back track or two when he spotted Detective Ford's cruiser—had him thinking that if he did look back he might crumble into a pile of salt only three inches tall. With all his running, he believed he had depleted that precious chemical compound from his body.

He jumped a fence, cut across a yard, and found himself on Mrs. Bartlett's street. The curtains on most homes were drawn, the sprinklers mysteriously quiet. The birds, tuckered out from yanking worms from lawns, rested on tree limbs, clotheslines, and TV antennas. The eerie quiet made Silver fear that police would soon appear on rooftops, behind bushes, and from manhole covers. He slowed to a walk, lips parched, and stopped to quench his thirst from Mrs. Bartlett's garden hose. He splashed his face with cold water and let it run down his back until goose bumps gathered on his arms.

Then he heard his name shouted: "Silver!"

Jason was yelling from up the street.

Silver dropped the garden hose and let the water run over his huaraches. He swallowed, a chicken bone of self-pity in his throat, at the sight of Jason. When was the last time someone yelled his name, and came running?

★

At 6:23, at the edge of Blanche and police brutality, at an on-ramp where Silver lectured Jason on the steadfast friendship of red ants (three of the little creatures provided a living example as they hauled away a toothpick), a teenage cowpoke braked his new Dodge Ram truck, sending up a cloud of dust and a "Yippee." The pimply driver hooked his thumb, relegating the two poets to the bed of the truck. It was all right by them.

They ate sandwiches that Jason, the true sponsor of their

adventure with a wallet packed with twenties, had bought at Subway, and snacked on apples while the truck descended the Tehachapi grade at eighty miles an hour. The apple's pulp flew out of their mouths, but they managed to swallow enough to feel satisfied.

"You know what tomorrow is?" Jason screamed into the windstorm created by the truck's hurtling speed. He had taken out the metal doodads and chrome ball from his tongue and tossed them overboard. He had become another person without them. Even his purplish dyed hair was beginning to blacken.

Silver, eyes reduced to mere slits in the harsh wind, shrugged.

"Tomorrow's Daylight Savings Time."

Silver mused on the hour they would lose. He brought out his notepad from his back pocket and wrote, "One less hour of this." For him, "this" was the life of unread poetry. Let America, he grumbled, watch TV and lose out.

They were left off near Weedpatch, ten miles southeast of Bakersfield, a little before eight in the evening, and soldiered over rock and sand a half a mile from the freeway. Silver argued that they had to keep out of sight of the CHP, who were always on the lookout for transients and poets on their way home.

Away from the stream of cars on the freeway, the night was black in the east and purplish in the west where the sun had gone down in the Pacific. The moon was white as a child's tooth. Stars shifted in the night sky, and Silver, an astronomer of new beginnings, predicted that their luck would change for the better. A coyote howled under the moon and stars, and Jason howled until Silver told him to be quiet or the coyotes might trot over and see who he was. Jason became big-eyed in the dark.

"I never slept on the ground before," Jason said. He was cutting a path for Silver through creosote bushes, ragweed, and manzanita bushes with antlerlike limbs.

"And you never will as long as you're with me."

The prediction was true. They slept that evening in a truly abandoned car—the motor was gone, the windshield, the radiator, and one door gone. In time, the entire vehicle would disappear if the scouring wind continued. They got comfy in the car, gritty with sand, and Silver pulled on his beard philosophically.

"Your generation's got a problem."

"What's that?" Jason asked. He passed a new bottle of water to Silver.

Silver took the bottle, cracked it, and sipped. "It's your names, Homes. You young people all sound alike. Like the poetry in this country."

Jason sipped on his bottle, downcast. He moistened his eyelids and scrubbed them with a finger.

Silver registered Jason's sadness. He slapped his young friend on the back and crowned him with a new name— same spelling but with Spanish pronunciation—"Ha-Són."

Jason smiled broadly. "That's cool." His eyes were mud from the scrubbing.

"We're going make you Chicano, *ese.*"

Jason repeated his new name until he fell asleep.

Silver was too jazzed to sleep. He studied the stars through the cracked window on the passenger's side. The moon had aged and was now yellow. His memory had returned, and he didn't want some of it—Detective Ford, for instance, and the little man in the black suit. Perhaps they could go away for good down that tunnel called Alzheimer's. Mrs. Bartlett was sweetly wrong, but bless her anyhow. He thought of them, and of Laura, whom he imagined snapping at Salvador to giddy up on a single-mattress bed. He thought of Elena and Larson, one of whom was living and the other dead. Still, they were friends.

They woke at what they assumed was first light but was control burning started by farmers. Silver massaged his neck and the small of his back, while Jason peed on a tire cracked with age. The tire blackened from his long, pouring fluids.

"How come they're making a fire?" Jason asked, zipping up. Fire flickered on the wetness of his eyes. He drank from his water bottle.

Silver couldn't answer him directly. "Oh, I guess they're mad about the price of cotton." He accepted the water bottle that Jason had passed him.

The wind picked up, suddenly, shifting the sand at their feet. From the hill a tumbleweed, sparked with fire, rolled their way, kicked along by wind. A second and third tumbleweed rolled toward them, and Silver kicked them aside. Then he remembered the prophecy of his dream, of his mother squirting lighter fluid on a tumbleweed, of a small gurgling spring, and a downed airplane in the dusty hills. The fire part was true, it seemed, and perhaps if they looked long enough they might find a single-engine airplane crashed in a gully.

"Let's go!" Silver called instinctively.

"Say my name, Silver," Jason begged. His backpack was slung on his shoulders, his steps matching Silver's long strides.

Silver had to smile in spite of another tumbleweed rolling past him. "Let's go, Ha-Són!"

The desert was on fire, and the two poets, one old and the other young, were running through it, carefully, for the journey was long and the rocks and potholes tricky on the ankles. Once you fell, Silver mused, there was no way of getting back up without a young man's help.   ★

DATE DUE

NOV 1 4 2013			
DEC 4 2013			
DEC 1 8 2013			
JAN 6 2014			